DEATH KNOCKS

THE SOUL HUNTERS -BOOK ONE

MIRANDA HARDY

JAY NOEL

4 Wing Press
St. Louis, Missouri

Edited by: Todd Barselow
Cover by: Thebookbrander.com

Death Knocks / Miranda Hardy and Jay Noel. —
Third Edition
ISBN 978-0-9912356-7-4 (Print Edition)

the Dark Projects

Visit www.thedarkprojects.com or www.jaynoel.com to find more exciting adventures featuring Urban Legends from around the globe.

M.H. ~ For Faith and Cody

J.N. ~ For Dom, Ally, and A.J.

"Pale death, with impartial step, knocks at the hut of the poor and the tower of kings." ~ Horace

MAVERICK

D EATH BY BEHEADING...by far the best way to go; it's final, quick, and undeniably messy.

"Bruh, you're 'bout to be slayed." The springs in the couch creak under the weight of my bouncing butt. The obnoxious noises that escape my lips sound like the heehaws a jackass makes, but my distraction technique works.

"Don't bet on it." Tarick's long thumbs click the buttons faster. He moves to the edge of the couch. "Dang it!" He hurls the game controller at me, and it hits my chest.

I shake an accusing finger at him. "Told you." I toss the controller back at Tarick, and it hits his bony shoulder. "Spending too much time with your girl; you got no fire left in you."

"Man, whatever. At least I have a girl." Tarick pushes up off the couch and heads a few feet towards the kitchen. "Soda?"

"Yeah." I nod without taking my eyes away from the video game on the screen—my medieval warrior beheads Tarick's character with one final slash of its sword.

"Okay, but you need to drink it in the kitchen. My mom's going ballistic lately about the rules." Tarick pops two soda cans open. "This morning she went bananas because flies were attacking her."

He snickers as he leaves the kitchen, and he sets my drink on the countertop. "She picked up the kitchen sponge and maggots were crawling all over it. She screamed like Leather Face was coming at her with a chainsaw. Woke the whole dang house. My dad charged out in boxers carrying a baseball bat." Tarick crouches down with one hand up holding an imaginary baseball bat. His nose scrunches up; it reminds me of a constipated old man.

I leave the comfort of the couch and grab my soda on the counter. "Your mom's crazy," I say before I take a giant gulp of soda.

"*My* mom?" Tarick's eyes widen. "At least she's not obsessed with *Top Gun, Maverick*. Your mom keeps calling me Goose, and I'm not even white."

"Low blow, T. That's not funny."

Mom must had been high at the hospital when she named me after that stupid guy. There should be a law against allowing moms hopped up on pain medication to name their babies. To this day, it's unbelievable my dad let her name me *Maverick*.

I take one final swig of my soda and hurry back to the couch.

"Sorry, I can't help myself." Tarick plops down next to me and moves the controller to the coffee table. "It is funny, by the way. Just be thankful she's not a *Star Wars* fan. Your name could be Obi Wan Kenobi."

"Yeah, yeah." I point to the controller. "Givin' up already?"

"How many times do you want to beat me?" He rolls his eyes. "Seriously, bruh...thanks." Tarick stretches his long arms across the back of the couch.

"Thanks? For what?" I lean back and fold my hands behind my head. "For beating your ass over and over again?"

Tarick's smile fades, and I can tell that he's going to say something serious.

"It's good to see you being yourself again, man," he says.

I know what he's getting at, but he's wrong. "What are you talking about?"

"The last few months, you've been acting a little weird. Not yourself." Tarick takes a deep breath. "I'm just saying I'm glad you're laughing and being your normal dumbass self, that's all."

I'm about to tell him that I've stopped taking my depression medication, but I decide to keep my mouth shut. This time, I'll control the darkness. Sure, the pills stopped me from falling deeper into that black hole, but it also made me feel so...blah.

Nothing. Like nothing mattered. I wasn't as sad with the pills, but I also wasn't as happy. I don't need any pills.

Tarick shakes his head. "And I know you could have gone to that party tonight. You didn't have to join my jail sentence." His serious side takes me by surprise. "I'm sure you'd rather be partying it up one last time before school starts instead of being stuck here with me on babysitting duty."

"Who wants to party with hot babes in bikinis anyway? I mean…this is so much better." I'm trying to keep a straight face, but I start to crack up. "Somebody's gotta make sure you don't get charged with child abuse. I may have taken that child development class last year so I could hang out with a bunch of girls, but I did learn a thing or two."

He grins sideways at me that lets me know he appreciates me not bailing on him to go to the big end of summer bash.

As if on cue, Tarick's baby sister wails from the other room.

"Now you gone and done it." Tarick darts toward the bedroom and comes back with Cally, or Little T, as I call her. He holds her with outstretched arms and wrinkles his nose. "She stinks worse than your feet."

"Why'd you bring her out here?"

Tarrick places her next to me on the couch. "Cause she wouldn't stop crying till I picked her up. Can you get me a diaper?"

"Seriously?" A powdery smell wafts up my nostrils

when I retrieve a diaper and wipes from Little T's room.

Tarick takes the wipes and smears the orangish, brown poop all over the baby's bottom with it. He's struggling, and her butt's not getting any cleaner. If anything, he's making it worse.

"Geez, Tarick, you should have taken that class with me. Pathetic."

Tarick holds Little T's legs up and twists her toward me. "Go for it, man. You're the expert."

I snatch the wipes from him. "Well, it sure isn't like the dolls we used in class." If the girls could see me now, maybe I'd nab a date or two.

Little T hardly struggles as I work to clean her up. I'm probably using way too many wipes, and stick them in a plastic bag one at a time after use. Tarick watches me carefully, as if he's trying to remember how I'm doing this. After I finish wiping away her poop, Tarick puts the new diaper under her and tapes one side while I tape the other side. I tie the plastic bag shut, and we stare at the stinky diaper on the coffee table. Little T opens her little mouth and starts to whine.

"Hand me that binky thing." Tarick points to where it fell out of Cally's mouth. "Hurry, plug her up."

"No, *you* pick up her binky. My hands are dirty."

"Mine are, too," Tarick protests.

"Mine are dirtier, since I did all the work cleaning her poop."

Tarick complies and picks up the yellow binky. He's about to put it in her mouth, but I shove him away with my shoulder.

"Dude, wash it first. That's nasty. You want something that's been on the floor to be stuck in *your* mouth?"

Tarick sighs and runs to the kitchen, then breaks into a sprint when her cries become bloody murder screams. Little T stops as soon as he puts the pacifier back in her mouth.

"Is she hungry or something?" I ask him.

Her legs kick when I scoop her up and hand her back to Tarick. He takes her in his arms and pats her back over his shoulder.

I say, "She's so much cuter when she's not screaming her head off. Lucky for her, she looks nothing like you."

He gives me a pretend kick to the shin. "Shut up. And no, she shouldn't be hungry. I fed her an hour ago, right before you got here."

She starts to whimper again.

Tarick is useless, so I hold out my arms. "Give her to me." He puts her back into my arms, and her crying stops. "See, she knows a good guy when she sees one."

Her pacifier squeaks as she sucks, and now she looks exhausted from all that screaming. Tarick wheels the bassinet into the living room with us, and I gently place her inside. She looks content now, and her tiny body wiggles before relaxing.

Tarick goes to the counter, picks up his soda, and takes another drink. "I will admit, that was pretty smooth. I'm glad you're here."

"Yeah, sure." I pick up the controller. "Another game?"

The television screen changes scenes to the different players, and an odd feeling overtakes me… the feeling that someone is watching me.

Silence falls between us as the room begins to darken. The light from the television dims to a soft glow. I'm thinking either the TV is broken or there's some kind of electrical problem going on. The picture flickers and the video game music stops and starts again, like the sound of a twisted backdrop to a horror movie.

My attention shifts to Tarick. His head turns toward the door, and he moves as if he's in slow motion. Drops of Tarick's soda slide down his chin and splatter on the floor just as the knocks begin. Three hollow booms echo through the room, like cannons going off in the distance—only they're less than five feet away. Tarick inches toward the door. His hand trembles as it moves towards the doorknob.

"Don't, Tarick." We both glare at the front door. "I have a bad feeling." The one single thought in my mind screams at me that opening the door would be a big mistake.

Tarick flashes a fake smile. "It's probably just a neighbor."

His words quiver as they exit his mouth. His face

morphs into a longer version of his round features. His eyes look closer together, and a deep crease forms between them. If I didn't know better, I'd say he just aged ten years.

Maybe something's wrong with me, and I'm seeing things. I'd read about how even young people can die of an aneurysm. I must be having one because the pressure builds up in my head as if I'm in an airplane and my ears need to pop. I feel faint.

Tarick remains still and stares at the door. I can tell he doesn't want to open it either, but for some weird reason, he can't help himself.

He takes another step towards the door, and his hand wraps around the doorknob. Any opportunity for me to protest fades. I don't know why, but I just have to know what's behind that door. Tarick shuts one eye and presses his right eye up against the peephole.

"Who's there?" I ask him.

Tarick cracks a nervous grin. "Oh man, it's just a kid."

"From the neighborhood?"

"Uh, I don't know," he replies. "He's got a hoodie on."

With shaking hands, Tarick unlocks the door and turns the doorknob. Its hinges creak as he pulls it open just an inch. A breeze sweeps in; the smell of flowers mixed with a musty, ancient scent fills the room.

I have the strongest urge to run and hide under

the covers as if I'm a little kid and there are monsters underneath my bed. Instead, my feet take me closer to Tarick. The crazy thought that these may be the last few steps of my life doesn't stop me from going up to him.

I have no idea why I'm so terrified of a kid in a hoodie.

Tarick opens the door a little more, and he looks down at whoever had been knocking. His dark skin blanches, the color of his now damp flesh becomes almost as light as my complexion.

At this point, I *know* I'm seeing things.

I peek around the doorframe and Tarick's shoulder to see the five-foot tall boy stare up through his hoodie at Tarick. His eyes lock onto Tarick's. His oversized clothes look like they belong on someone two feet taller and a lot rounder. Baggy jeans sag around the kid's bony legs, and the sweatshirt hides his hands. He pushes one sleeve up to reveal the whitest hand I've ever seen.

"May I enter to use the phone? I'm lost," the boy asks, his voice demanding, yet soft and innocent.

He faces me and that's when I see the solid black spheres that are his eyes. His pupils hide the white that should be there...somewhere. My hand grabs Tarick's arm and squeezes to let him know to shut the door. My tongue feels so heavy in my mouth that it becomes difficult—no, impossible—to utter a single word.

As I'm staring at this bug-eyed boy, Tarick's bicep

hardens under my grip, and the side of the door softly cracks from his grasp. He can't seem to look away from the alien-looking boy, and neither can I.

The hair on my arms stand up, and my heartbeat thrums in my ears like a sixteen piece percussion set. The monsters under the bed were nothing compared to the black orbs on this kid's face. My mouth, legs, and arms betray me. My mind tells me to yell, shut the door, and run like hell, but my limbs feel like Jell-O. Time stands still, and the realization that I'm about to die invades me.

My best friend's mouth opens, but nothing comes out. His hands start to shake again as his chin reluctantly dips once. Tarick just invited this monster in! The stranger no longer seems like a kid to me. He's a predator.

I want to yell at Tarick to shut the door, but I can't speak. My nails dig into Tarick's arm in my attempt to pull him away. My legs back up against the couch and the kid pushes in, lowers his hood, and reveals a full head of shaggy blond hair. I expected this demon child to have horns. Instead, his greasy hair covers his ears and hangs just below his neck.

Tarick backs up and knocks me over the edge of the couch. I can't control my body from tumbling backwards. My throat constricts to try to unleash a scream, but I've lost my voice.

The boy stands completely still, but Tarick falls to his knees, throws his face upwards, and his own unblinking eyes darken. My legs fly up into the air and my butt hits the tile floor. I begin to crawl backwards. This *thing* might have a pair of legs and arms, but I'm sure he's not human at all, and he somehow has a mental grip on Tarick.

There's no other way to explain what's happening.

Drops of blood trickle out of Tarick's ears. He raises his hand to wipe the blood, and it smears across his face. He pulls his gaze from the boy and stares at his own bloody hand. He turns to look at me. His bottom lip quivers, and a ring of crimson spreads under the brown in his eyes. Tarick can't speak either, but he mouths one word...*Cally*.

The evil being turns his attention to me, and as he does so, his blackness penetrates my head. "Stay." My body immediately goes rigid, and my limbs become instantly paralyzed.

Why can't I control my own body?

He turns toward Cally and my adrenaline pumps through my veins. My face turns hot. The pressure in my head, along with the ringing in my ears, subside just enough for me to command my body to move. My limbs obey, and as the demon boy approaches the bassinet, I slam into him.

We crash into the wall hard. My face is inches from his, and his deep black eyes grow wide. He's just as surprised as I am at the violence of my hit.

Anger spreads on his face. Both of his hands strike my chest so hard that the air swooshes from my lungs. My feet leave the floor, and my whole body hurls backwards into the air. The sofa softens my fall, but my right leg smashes into the glass coffee table, shattering it.

Cally wails. The monster stands over her, and he licks his lips. "Too soon…maybe."

The sight of this thing staring at Cally gets my heart pumping again, and I'm back on my feet. Even if I'm willing to die, there's no way this creature's going to take Tarick's sister. My fists clench, and I'm ready to tear the bastard apart.

The black-eyed boy glides towards me like a ghost floating on air. My limbs release the built up tension, and I'm unable to tear my gaze from his eerie stare. My head pounds again. The ringing returns, immediately followed by a loud buzzing. The sound grows louder the closer he gets to me, and the agony in my head overpowers me.

I fall to my knees. A swarm of bees invade my brain; they multiply and begin to sting me from the inside out. The pressure builds up just behind my eyeballs and releases with a pop, and a wet substance slides down my cheek. I'm sure that my head has literally exploded, but I'm unable to scream.

Is Cally safe?

Tarick is still on his knees, looking up at the ceiling like he's in some kind of trance. I still can't even manage to say one word. My throat strains, and my ears pick up an eerie silence as the buzzing dissipates. I'm so dizzy that I fall over, and a thin layer of static blankets my eyesight.

Out of the corner of my eye, I can see the black-eyed monster come towards me with one had raised in the air. My last thought is of Cally and Tarick and how I had failed to protect them. The creature's pale fingers float towards my temple, and with the touch of cold flesh, the finality of darkness surrounds me.

2

MAVERICK

SOMETHING COLD TOUCHES my face. It brushes my chin and glides upward, like it's wiping crumbs away from my cheek. The blurry haze fades as my eyes blink it away, and a renewed terror grips me. A pair of black holes stare down at me. My head smashes into something as I attempt to back away. The sharp pain above my neck gives way to rapid throbbing that matches my hyper-fast heartbeat.

The taste of blood forms in my mouth, and I spit it out.

"Not real. This is not real." It's no good. The pain in my wrists tells me otherwise. Ropes bind my hands to something above me, and the numbness gives way to a stinging sensation.

The noisy bees return to my brain. Instead of an entire hive swarming, it's like there's only ten of them buzzing around. A pale, blond, black-eyed girl leans against a wall of old wooden planks a few feet away. She tilts her head and her gaze bores into me.

"Wh…wh…who?" My voice increases an octave. A million questions form in my mind, but my clouded head jumbles the words into unintelligible gibberish.

She smiles and pats her chest, like she's answering my question, but no words escape her mouth. Blood covers her hands—dried blood—and the memory of the hand brushing my face snaps into my brain. It's my blood on her hands.

Her dark eyes, identical to the stranger that had forced his way into Tarick's house, return my stare. No, wait…Tarick actually let that creature in. The fog starts to lift and my memories return. How could I forget the big black eyes? As if she knows her weird face freaks me out, she backs away.

"What are you?" I ask her.

My bravery returns, and I struggle against the ropes strangling my wrists.

Her attempt at friendliness, if that's what her smile means to be, fades and she moves toward me. Her mostly normal looking face droops. Although her hair color and pale skin are identical to the other black-eyed kid, she appears older. Smeared dirt stains her gray sweatshirt and sweatpants. If her face wasn't so clean and her hair straight and untangled, I'd think she'd belong in a homeless shelter.

I cringe and try to scoot back further, but pipes block my way. The ropes wrap around the plumbing under a sink. She takes another step forward and moves her crimson-stained hand closer to my face.

"Ssstay away!" My wrists feel like they catch fire as I pull hard, but they don't budge.

She stops her approach, thank God.

There's only darkness beyond the barely lit space. The single lit bulb dangles from the ceiling above the girl. Insects fly all around it. Cement block poles hold up the wooden walls. Although I see nothing in the distance, rain pounds the roof and the musty scent of wet earth fills the room.

How did I get here? Wasn't I just at Tarick's house?

"Where are my friends? Where's Tarick? Where's Cally?"

The girl turns toward the barn's entrance and then twirls her straight blonde hair around her pale finger. She bites down on her bottom lip. Once she stops twisting her hair, she takes yet another step forward. The swarm of bees in my head returns with a vengeance.

I struggle again. "Stop!"

Fear takes root, as if it's slowly eating away at my soul. None of this makes sense and my instincts yell at me to run, but these ropes won't budge. I try yanking down hard, but it's no good. The buzzing in my brain eases when she retreats and keeps her distance.

She paces back and forth, no longer intent on coming near me.

"Answer me, damnit! Where are my friends?"

Confusion, and then a sympathetic look, spreads on her face. She stops to look at me and tilts her head again. Her black eyes won't stop staring at me, and now I know what it's like to be a caged animal at the zoo. She swoops forward and bends down to pull at the ropes. I swallow my panic. What is she doing?

She doesn't seem to hold the same power over me that the black-eyed boy had. I'm able to squirm away from her. She quits yanking and slides her cold hand down my cheek. She smiles, and goose bumps form on my arms.

A shiver passes through me. My brain shakes itself of the cobwebs and the buzz dissolves. My thoughts turn razor sharp.

Where is the black-eyed boy? Tarick must be prisoner elsewhere. I'm desperate to get out of here and find Tarick and Cally.

She shakes her head and mumbles something incomprehensible. Is it another language, or is she completely doped up? If a certain drug can mess up your eyes like that…that's something to stay clear of. There's no color, no eyeballs, just blackness. My instincts tell me it's not drug induced, and the best thing to do is stay far away. She pulls at the rope again, and it comes undone. My arms fall and I slump forward to the ground.

I'm free.

The cold cement floor feels good to my numb limbs, but I manage to push myself up. Other than my arms and legs feeling like they're being poked by pins and needles, I seem to be relatively okay.

Instead of attacking me, the girl moves to the open door of the pole barn with such absolute silence, I'm freaked out. Either she's a ghost or she's a ninja. She points into the rainy darkness beyond the open doorway.

She's letting me go?

I'm not going to give her the chance to change her mind. The downpour pelts my body when I run outside. I trip over a bump in the cement, and my sore limbs meet the dirt, along with half of my left cheek. My hands find the muddy earth before my face becomes wedged into the soft mush. Bits of mud splash into my open mouth. I reach out and my hand finds something that feels like a dead dog or horse.

Through the heavy rain, I stare at the mud-covered form. It takes several seconds for my brain to finally register what I'm looking at. It's a body… Tarick's bloody face half pressed into the mud, one bloodshot eye staring blankly at me. A cockroach races across his forehead.

"Tarick!"

Maybe he's just unconscious.

"Oh God! Oh God!"

I wrap my arms around him and cradle him. His body slips from my grasp and collapses back into the mud.

He's gone.

The black-eyed girl kneels next to me, a blank expression plastered on her face.

I almost shove her away, but I'm afraid to touch her. "Stay away from me!"

Tarick lies in the mud. A cry builds from the depths of my belly and erupts out of my lips.

She opens her mouth and screeches like a dying cat. The sound jolts me backwards, and my instincts kick in. I fumble as I rise, and then I turn and run.

Massive rain drops pound me and mix with my tears. With each pump of my legs, the guilt builds inside of me. I should turn around and get Tarick, but fear drives me to run away instead.

The ground becomes mushy under my flip-flops; the mud threatens to swallow my feet. My toes clutch the rubber straps to keep them from flying off, and I finally reach the grass next to the dirt road.

Even from fifty yards away, I can still see the strange girl standing at the edge of the pole barn. She lingers over Tarick's body. She looks up at me and waves her hand like she's saying goodbye after a friendly visit.

Astid. My name's Astid. A female voice rings loud in my mind, as if the volume of the television has reached maximum volume.

What was that?

In a mad panic, I swivel around and take off again. As I'm running, I can't shake the image of Tarick's hollow eyes. I want to turn back, but I just can't. Remorse spreads into my stomach, its acid touching my tongue. The urge to throw up becomes too strong, and the vomit flows over into the dirt. The retching makes my eyes feel as if they're going to pop out of my skull. My stomach continues to pump even though there's nothing left to spew.

My lungs twinge, and my breath increases in short spurts before I force my legs to move again. Running next to the mud path keeps me free of the trees. The buzz in my head fades the more distance I put between myself and that freaky girl. When the light of the barn's solitary light bulb no longer shines behind me, the bees disappear from my head altogether.

The grassy path crosses at a bigger dirt road. I pick up the pace. My tears sting my eyes, making it tough to focus on the road. This monsoon isn't helping.

But wait...what if the boy-monster is here? My new found fear drives me to push harder. I have to stay aware of my surroundings and keep an eye out for the black-eyed demon.

Where's the police when you need them?

A bright gleam peeks through the treetops, and my stride quickens. The street light is a welcome sight, but the speeding truck that flies by on the paved road makes my heart leap with utter joy. The road looks familiar. My mind begins to clear finally.

Okay, now I know where I am. My breathing slows down, and my brain finally snaps into reality.

Sort of.

When I was tied up with that creepy girl, I could have sworn I was on the other side of the world. But I was just a couple miles from home. In fact, that old unfinished pole barn has been there as long as I can remember, but I never paid much attention to it before.

The truck's taillights become less visible in the distance and not another vehicle is in sight. Since my brain isn't foggy, I check my pants for my phone. I need to call the cops and get a whole SWAT team to take down the black-eyed duo. My phone's not there.

Shivering from the chill of the rain, running the last two miles to my development just about kills me, and I curse the fact we had moved so far from town. Not one car goes by me on my trek. Each second that passes means that Tarick's body remains in that mud, all by himself. My chest aches, and I hold back more tears that want to burst free.

Although it isn't much further, my limbs feel as if I've run for hours. The street lights increase in number the closer I get to my subdivision. I keep running on the grass, near the foliage. The pain in my body radiates and demands that I quit, but I push forward.

My thoughts go over the night's events, over and over, but the image of Tarick's face in the mud haunts me. What am I going to say to his parents? That black-eyed aliens killed him? Oh God! And what about Cally? She's just a baby.

Unbelievably, I speed up. Please. Let the baby be okay.

If I hadn't seen the demon-boy for myself, I'd believe he only existed in the mind of Stephen King...and that evil sister, Astid—worse than a blood splattered *Carrie*. *Astid*. That's her name, right? Or was my brain going crazy from the strange bees buzzing in my head. She did let me go, but she's still one of *them*.

They will both pay for what they've done.

Finally, the sign for Bella Terra comes into view. The storm has died down, but it's still raining a little. A flashing patrol car zooms by, and the cop ignores my waves and pleas to stop. I pick up a rock and hurl it at the squad car, hoping to get his attention. But he's around the corner before the rock hits the pavement.

"Damnit!"

My footsteps slow as my brain tries to process the scene in the neighborhood. Mom stands outside our house and greets the officer after he gets out of his car. All the neighbors linger outside of their homes; some of them wander toward my house.

A hand grabs my shoulder, and my heart nearly leaps out of my chest. The moment I hear my own hideous scream, I'm immediately ashamed.

"Mav, what's your problem?"

Marcus, the neighborhood doper, sports a sideways grin and backs away from me.

"What's going on, man?" He jerks his head in the

direction of my house. "Boy, you is dirty." He looks me up and down. "Your eyes are redder than mine. What you been up to?"

"Maverick!" Mom shrieks and runs toward me, followed by the cop and Tarick's parents.

Mom collides into me and hugs me more tightly than she ever has before. She squeezes me so hard that it pushes the air from my lungs. "Oh, thank God! Thank God you're alright."

My body stiffens. "Mom, I'm fine. I…"

"Where's Tarick?" his mom asks. She approaches us and scans the road behind me for signs of her son. Cally clings to her hip, and my relief overwhelms me.

I collect myself before I try to answer her. "He's…" Tears cloud my vision.

His mother's slim, sweet face looks hopeful, and I can't tell her what happened. All of that guilt hits me hard. I should have stayed with Tarick.

I'm such a coward.

Everyone's staring at me, waiting for my reply. My mom's grip on my shoulders tighten.

"He's dead," I whisper. "They killed him."

3

ASTID

E HEARD ME. He turned when I sent my name to his mind. I'm not sure why I even tried to reach out to him in the first place, since I was told that the human brain wasn't normally receptive to our communications. He was just so...afraid, I wanted to comfort him.

It makes me think that I can communicate with humans in this way, which gives me hope.

Maverick. His name sounds wonderful and exotic in my mind.

His muddy brown shirt disappears as he turns toward the road. Even though the craving to follow him beckons me, the risk is too high. Staying here is no longer an option either. Kren will be back soon, and I don't want to be subjected to his fury. He will know what I have done, and he won't understand why I let Maverick go.

My instincts nearly took over when Maverick

first opened his eyes, and it took all of my strength not to take him. Despite what the others say, it is possible to suppress the hunger. It is possible to send thoughts to their minds.

Kren's anger and insistence will not sway me to take another life. This time, he will deal with my decisions.

Kren will have no choice.

Maverick's feelings upset me deeply. The waves of horror and sadness radiated from his aura, and the magnitude of such emotions astounded me. Touching Maverick's mind almost hurt me. Flashes of his inner essence produced fleeting pieces of a range of emotions. Joy, fear, happiness, anger, friendship, and finally...mourning for the loss of his companion. His life felt both terrifying and magnificent.

Such a full and rich existence, yet he longed...

What have you done? Kren interrupts my peaceful thoughts. He stands at the edge of the cement shelter, dripping wet from the rain. He stares at the ropes still dangling from the metal.

I did what I needed to do. I gather my strength as I approach my angry brother, placing my hand on his shoulder. *You knew I would refuse. You knew this would happen.*

Kren turns to look out into the darkness.

It's too late. My hand grips his shoulder tighter. *He's gone.*

How could you? What were you thinking? Kren's eyes

narrow. *He'll bring others.*

Then we shouldn't be here when they come.

Kren shrugs my hand away. *Why do you have to be so stubborn? I was trying to save you.* His anger gives way to compassion. *You'll die because of this.*

I know.

Kren's hands roll up into fists, and he paces back and forth. He finally stops and glares at me as if he's decided on something. *You stay here. We will find you more. The one outside is no longer a viable option. I'll dispose of him myself.*

There's a new look in his eyes, something beyond anger. It's desperation. Kren loves me, yet a part of him despises me. He cares so much, he's willing to do anything to keep me alive. But he won't let me make my own decisions.

My tense shoulders loosen, and my head bows low. *I understand, but we must move from this place. I'll meet you two miles south in the open field.*

Kren throws me one final accusing look over his shoulder before he leaves with the body. He lifts the limp body of Maverick's friend with ease, a feat that would be difficult for me now. My mind's defenses shut out Kren's attempt to touch it.

My deepest desires stay hidden.

A chill from the cold air makes me shiver. The thick raindrops continue to fall. When Kren comes back, he will not find me waiting in that field. He is sure to hunt for me, but I will stay hidden long enough for him to have to abandon his search.

Soon, the others will be coming, and it won't be safe for any of us.

4

MAVERICK

T ARICK'S GONE.
The muddy spot where his body lay just an hour ago looks as if nothing was there. I'm careful to retrace my steps from the barn, and I'm sure this was the spot. "He was here. I swear he was here."

The cops comb the entire area. A police dog sniffs all around, but pulls his handler in too many directions. The officer attached to the leash looks frustrated and shakes his head.

"You're sure this is where your friend was?" The bulky, bald officer presses his lips tightly.

"That's what I told you." I don't like how the cop looks at me with a suspicious eye. My irritation is on the verge of becoming a full blown meltdown. "He was laying right there. They must have taken him somewhere."

The rain stopped a few minutes ago, but the musty

air is thick with humidity. Cops exit the barn and one of them tells another officer that they didn't even find the ropes that had *allegedly* bound my hands to the pipe.

Am I still dreaming? Maybe if we go back to Tarick's house, we'll find him safe and sound in his room. But this is all real. This is really happening. Tarick is dead, and now we can't find his body.

Mom squeezes my hand and pulls me to her. She uses her other hand to rub my back. "They'll find him."

Tarick's dad, Mr. Lester, stands on the other side of the officer, but his wife waits in the car with Cally. He's motionless and just stares at me without uttering a word. I know what he's thinking. He's thinking that this is all my fault.

Loud sirens replace the normal night sounds, and an ambulance pulls onto the dirt driveway.

"Let's get you to the hospital," the officer says, holding up his arm and trying to guide me toward the ambulance.

"I don't need to go to the hospital." I reach out to my mom. "I'm fine. I need to help look for Tarick."

Her grasp tightens. "Maverick, please let them look at you."

"There's nothing wrong with me."

"We just need to make sure, honey." She wipes my face and holds it between her hands. "Please do this for me."

Everyone stares at me. Not one facial expression

offers any kind of sympathy. I already abandoned Tarick once, I'm not ready to do it again.

"Why is no one listening to me? Tarick is out there." I point toward the dense woods. "We need to find him, damnit!"

I jerk myself free from my Mom's grasp, and she almost loses her balance as I make a run for it. The officer springs on me before I can get too far. Another cop joins him, and then the paramedic joins in. My adrenaline kicks in, and my reflexes take over before my mind comprehends what's happening. All three men hold me down, and my strength leaves me. They drag me towards the ambulance as my struggles prove useless.

"Kid, what did you take tonight?" the male paramedic asks.

They think I'm on drugs? "Nothing, you asshole."

Despite my kicking and protests, they strap me down to the gurney and push me into the open emergency vehicle. They direct Mom to the front passenger seat. She cries but struggles to keep it together.

"Is he on any medication?" the female paramedic asks my mom.

She nods and lists off the depression medicine I'm *supposed* to be taking. Are they going to run blood tests and find out that I've been skipping out on my meds? This just gets better and better.

"You've got a nasty cut," the lady says as she tends

to the wound on my forehead. "Might need a few stitches."

The double doors close, and the lady wraps my arm with one of those blood pressure things. She puts the stethoscope into her ears and puts some clip-thingy on my finger. The cuff tightens against my bicep while she inflates the wrap with the rubber ball in her hand.

"Does he have a history of hypertension or rapid heartbeat?" the short haired, butch lady asks Mom.

"No," she replies. "Why?"

The vehicle bounces around and veers to the right before it hits smooth pavement.

The paramedic removes the stethoscope and unwraps my arm. "His blood pressure is high, and his pulse is racing. But then again, considering the circumstances, that's to be expected."

I don't like how they're talking about me as if I'm not here.

She bends over me to shine a light in my right eye.

"That thing's bright," I protest.

She pulls up the lid to my left eye and blinds me with her flashlight. When she's done, all I can see are these big purple dots floating around, and it takes a while for them to disappear. When my vision returns, the paramedic's facial expression indicates she has found something wrong with me.

"What is it?" If my blood pressure was taken now, it'd shoot through the roof.

"You have some blood vessels ruptured in both eyes. Were you struck in the eye or anything?"

Bees buzzed in my head and the black-eyed kids tried to kill me, but that's all. I don't remember actually being hit in the eyes. "No."

"It's no big deal, usually," she says. "You can burst an eye vessel by just sneezing or coughing really hard. Even stress can cause a vessel to hemorrhage."

The driver talks about me into his radio. He gives my physical description, something about me being stable, and that I'm coming in with Mom. We're just a few minutes or miles away.

"Does he have a history of drug use? Alcohol consumption?" the woman asks Mom.

Mom swivels around and glances at me as she wipes a fresh tear from her face. "No. Not at all."

The paramedic rubs my left arm with an alcohol pad. She peels open a small package to reveal something that looks like a big ass needle.

"What are you doing?" My arms tighten, but the straps keep me immobile.

Her fingers press against my arm. "I need to start an IV. You are severely dehydrated."

"I don't want anything that's going to knock me out or anything."

She drops her chin and looks me straight in the eyes. "I'm only going to give you some fluids. We need to keep you hydrated. This is just a small catheter, so you'll feel just a little pinch, that's all."

She punctures my vein, and it only burns for a

second. After taping the little plastic thing to my arm, she connects a tube to a bag containing clear fluid and then attaches it to my IV. An icy chill creeps up my arm.

My eyes close, and I take deep breaths and try my best to relax. The trip to the hospital seems like it takes hours, but we arrive maybe twenty minutes later. The doors open and they roll me out. The sky remains dark. A warm wind caresses my body, gives me goose bumps, and brings the scent of wet earth to my nostrils.

They wheel my gurney into the emergency room lobby where a nurse gets all the information from the pair of paramedics. The nurse takes Mom aside. I can't hear what they're saying, and every now and then Mom glances over at me.

I'm still angry about having to leave the search for Tarick. Mr. and Mrs. Lester probably think the worst of me. I keep waiting for the police to show up at the hospital, but it's a good sign that they're not around. When they find Tarick's body, all fingers will point to me.

The urge to throw up seizes my stomach again, but I swallow the acid and struggle to keep it down.

The term 'subconjunctival hemorrhage' comes from the lady paramedic that talks to Mom, and she repeats that it's, "No big deal."

"Will his eyes get better? Will it affect his eyesight?" Mom asks.

"No, they will clear up within ten to fourteen days

on their own. There's no signs of head trauma or concussion."

They continue their talk, but the words don't make sense to me.

The male EMT leaves the nurse and looks down at me. "We're going to transfer you to a regular hospital bed. You're going to cooperate, right? We don't want to strap you down any more than you want us to."

"I promise to be good," I reply.

It's yet another good sign that they don't intend to handcuff me to a bed.

"Maverick?" Mom calls to me as she approaches my stretcher. "They will probably just keep you overnight to keep an eye on you." She wraps her arms around me. "There's no need to worry. We'll figure all of this out together."

They undo the straps around my arms and legs. I try to keep it together, but I just lose it. My body convulses and I can't stop from sobbing into Mom's arms.

THE NIGHT in the hospital felt like an evening in Hell. The only thing missing was the fire, pitchforks, and drunk dancing demons. Who could possibly sleep with the constant interruptions and beeps? Mom, however, was able to pass out and sleep through most of the night. In fact, she's still out in the uncomfortable fake leather, brown chair.

But for me, there was no way to get more than a couple hours of sleep. The night nurse made an appearance every three hours, took blood from me a few times, always for one test or another. It's ridiculous the amount of useless tests they run in the hospital. They think my system will test positive for drugs, but they will be disappointed.

Every time the door to my room opened, I half-expected it to be a cop to give us an update about Tarick. Maybe it's a good thing that I'm here. I don't think I could handle seeing his dead body like that again.

The morning sunrise peeks through the window blinds. Directly across from me is the empty bed. Mom refused to sleep in it even though the nurse offered.

Being in the hospital is nothing like it is on TV or in the movies. I never thought that you had to have a freaking roommate in the hospital. That's gross. The one place you don't want a roommate is in the hospital. The other person could snore, fart up a storm, or even talk in their sleep.

Tarick would crack a joke about old people who fart all the time, if he were here.

I hear the sound of feet scampering outside my room. Two voices whisper right by my closed door. They don't whisper too softly, so I can make out everything they're saying.

"Did you test for various drugs?" a deep voice asks.

"Yes, that's protocol, but you'll need a warrant in order to get the results," another male voice answers.

The loudspeaker crackles on, and the static makes it impossible to decipher what they're saying. I lean over in my weak attempt to eavesdrop, but it's still no use. Are they doctors or cops out there talking about me?

I'm starting to freak out, and I'm so aggravated, I want to jump out of bed and tell them to talk about me to my face. The stupid intercom finally shuts off, and I can hear their conversation again.

The deep voice continues, "The other teen hasn't been found, and we're expecting the worst. That kid is now our prime suspect."

5

MAVERICK

T HE FOG ON the bathroom mirror evaporates when I push open the door. The alien reflection stares back at me. Jagged stitches on my head remind me of Frankenstein. My hair feels greasy since the doctor strictly forbade me—under penalty of what I'm not sure—from washing it properly. I'm not one to check myself out in the mirror a lot, but I feel like I'm looking at somebody else as I stare at my jacked up face.

My eyes look like they are something out of a horror movie…the demon bad guy who gets ready to devour the town of innocent victims. Red streaks surround my brown irises. Purple bruises frame my ears, which are still very sore. No wonder that cop called me the prime suspect. The deranged monster that stares back at me looks capable of luring children into its lair and eating them.

Although it's wonderful to be out of the hospital,

my own room feels foreign to me. At least there are no cops here bugging me. Back in the hospital, Mom wouldn't let me answer any of the cop's questions, although I have nothing to hide. Her rudeness to the cop shocked me. Mom's usually a mellow person. A worrier. She refused to allow me to go to the station and told him to send out an investigator to the house so I'd have time to heal.

The walls of my room close in on me. I'm not in jail, or even at the police station, but I've exchanged one prison for another. Mom made it clear I'm not allowed to leave the house until school starts, and even then, only to go to school and come right back home.

At first I'm pissed about being punished, but then I think about Tarick. His parents must be going out of their minds, and I'm stuck in here…helpless. Mom won't let me reach out to them, which is probably for the best. Since I'm the unofficial prime suspect, I'm sure that Tarick's mom and dad don't want me around anyway.

The phone on my nightstand buzzes again. Even people that aren't really my friends have been calling. Most of the messages were from concerned class-mates offering their prayers or best wishes. A handful are from those who think I killed my best friend. They're the ones that tell me that I will burn in Hell or rot in jail. Or both.

This time, it's a text message from Cadence:
Mav, seriously, call me ASAP. Worried about Tarick.

Followed by:

His parents aren't talking to me. WTF is going on Mav?

What am I supposed to say to her? Obviously, word has gotten around. Big mouth Marcus spreads news faster than the reporters could get the story out. Eventually, I'll have to reply to Cadence. She's Tarick's girlfriend after all. But for now, I just want the covers to swallow me. The nightstand drawer continues to buzz next to my bed.

The heat from the bathroom spreads into my room, and the open window helps circulate the air. It's not much hotter outside, but Mom will come in soon and tell me to shut the window since we can't afford to air condition the entire world.

My mattress bounces from my weight, and my head sinks into the pillow. Mom's voice carries from down the hall. Sounds like she's on the phone. I crane my neck to catch what she's saying.

"No, they haven't. They put out an Amber Alert on him this morning, so his picture is up all over the news channels."

That's why she's not letting me watch television.

"What should I do? Call and hire a lawyer?" she asks. "No, they are sending over a detective to ask questions at about two o'clock."

The clock on the nightstand reads 1:50. Crap. That's all I need.

"Charles, you have no idea how this is affecting me. I'm in the dark and I don't know what to do."

Great. She's talking with Dad. Well, at least she's not yelling. The two were hardly civil when they were married, and they sure didn't get along any better after the divorce.

"Fine. I will. I'll call you later. Goodbye."

The phone thumps against its receiver and she sighs. Or maybe that's a yawn. All of this can't be easy on her either.

"Maverick?" Mom walks down the hall as I shut the window.

"Yeah?"

She stops in my doorway and stares at me. "How are you feeling?"

"I'm fine, Mom."

"Still achy? Do you need another pain pill?" she asks.

"No, that will just knock me out, and I'd rather not spend the rest of the day sleeping."

"Okay. Do you want something to eat? Probably soup is best."

"Sure."

I plop back down on my bed and the ceiling popcorn looks like tiny mountains. I begin to count the crevices under the white paint. She lingers at the edge of my room for a few awkward moments. Mom wants to check my arms for cuts, I'm sure of it, but she turns away before heading back towards the kitchen. I know my depression has been tough on her, and now she's probably terrified that I'm cutting again or maybe worse…that I'll do something more permanent.

My phone vibrates again. Is there a limit to the amount of messages one phone can hold before it won't allow any more? Probably not, and I'll be reading texts for the next week. At least the phone calls have stopped.

My eyes start to feel heavy and sleep threatens to take me, so I walk to the kitchen and sit at the table while Mom stirs the soup.

"Want some crackers?" she asks, and places them right in front of me.

The crackers taste like heaven compared to the hospital breakfast from this morning. Someone put in great effort to make the eggs taste like rubber. The grits were worse. That crap could spackle the little cracks in my ceiling. I'm sure I've lost a pound or two just in the last day, between the horrible hospital food and a lack of appetite.

"There's a detective coming over soon to talk with us," Mom says with her back toward me as she pours the soup into a bowl.

She scoops out the chicken pieces. To me, that is not real chicken. The can says it's chicken, but we all know what type of meat that really is…ground up junk that no one else wants to eat. Probably chicken parts like bones, eyeballs, and brains.

"I know." The dry cracker courses down my throat. "I heard you talking to Dad."

"Oh." She places the soup in front of me and goes to the freezer. She plops the ice cube into the bowl.

"I'm not a little kid, Mom. I can cool down my own soup."

"Sorry."

The doorbell chimes through the house, and I'm so startled, I drop my spoon into the bowl. Mom rushes to the living room to answer it, and I restrain myself from telling her not to open the door.

"He's early," Mom says, as I see her looking out of the peephole. Our open floor plan doesn't leave room to hide anywhere.

Part of me thinks it's ridiculous to be afraid of doorbells and door knocks, but I can't help but remember the black-eyed boy stepping into Tarick's house. The way he looked at baby Cally, as if she was a meal to devour, and what he did to Tarick. The grotesque memory crashes back, and I feel nauseous.

"Hello," Mom says as she opens the door.

"Mrs. Ashe?" a deep, male voice asks.

"Yes."

"I'm Detective Drake Jennings. I spoke with you on the phone." He flashes his badge. "I hope this is a good time."

"Yes, please come in."

I get up from my chair and leave my soup. The detective seems closer to my mom's age. His dark skin glistens from the humid air making him sweat. I can tell that this guy's smart, and that he's all business. Reminds me of a drill sergeant, but in a suit.

"Thank you, Mrs. Ashe. Again, I apologize for my colleague's brash behavior in the hospital. He stepped out of bounds with trying to question your son there."

Mom motions for him to sit on the loveseat. He places folders on the coffee table and repositions his badge on his belt before sitting down. His holstered pistol peeks through his jacket.

"It's not your place to apologize for someone else's behavior, Detective." Mom sits down across from him and doesn't offer him anything to drink.

She also didn't shake his hand when he introduced himself. My mother is definitely not acting like herself.

I feel weird being the only one standing, so I plop down next to Mom.

Jennings says, "Well, I'm just sorry you had to deal with that while your son was trying to get well."

She nods, but I know she's not buying it.

He lifts the folder and opens it. "Is Maverick doing okay now?" He looks up from the papers.

Why don't adults just talk to me directly? It's annoying. "I'm doing fine."

He doesn't look at all caught off-guard, but he studies my face for too long. "That's great. Glad to hear you are doing better." He shuffles through more of his papers and slides the pen from one of his folders. "Well, it sounds like quite an ordeal you went through the other night."

Mom remains silent and watches him with suspicious eyes.

"I'm Detective Jennings, Maverick. It's nice to meet you." He extends his hand and I shake it. "I've been assigned to the case, and I want to do everything I can to find Tarick. We're searching for him everywhere at this very moment. Tracking dogs, volunteers, police officers—every resource available to us. But I need more information about last night. Hopefully, you'll be able to give us more clues."

"Detective Jennings, if you want to help us, then why aren't you out looking for Tarick?" I ask, a bit peeved at his attempt at pleasantries. "I've told my story several times to your officers and they didn't take anything I said seriously."

"I know you did. I also noted the consistency of your accounts. You mentioned some kids that showed up at the Lester residence, and they abducted you."

His obvious attempt to get me to tell him a different account of the same story irritates me. Valedictorian may not be in my future, but I'm not that stupid.

"There was no *they*, Detective. One black-eyed boy knocked on Tarick's door. Just one. I blacked out and ended up in the barn, where the other black-eyed girl was. She let me go. I tripped over Tarick's body, and then he was gone when the cops brought me back. That's it. That's all I have to say."

"Black-eyed kids?"

"Yes! They had solid black eyes. Can't be too hard to find them. You'd notice these two in a second. There was no white at all in their eyes. Just black." The acid bubbling up my throat threatens to bring up what little soup went down.

"Are you sure about this?" Jennings was impossible to read. His lean face looked like stone.

"Yes."

"And you were at Tarick's house just babysitting his little sister, Cally, right? The two of you were only playing video games. And that's all. Is it possible that maybe you and Mr. Lester were doing something that you shouldn't have been doing and imagined these black-eyed kids?"

"Detective Jennings, are you suggesting that they were on drugs?" Mom asks. She looks like she's ready to throw him out, but I know even she's not bold enough to do that. "You think my son and Tarick were high?"

"Mrs. Ashe, my job is to look at all the possibilities. Leave no stone left unturned."

I've had enough. "Not all teenagers are on drugs. I think I've told you all that I can, Detective."

Without another word, I get up from the couch and walk down the hall. I slam my door shut and lean the back of my head against it. The soreness from my bruises kicks in. Damnit!

After a few minutes, I press my ear against the door.

"I didn't mean to upset him, but I have to ask these questions as a part of the investigation."

"I know it's your job, but I know for a fact that Tarick and Maverick aren't on drugs. They tested my son at the hospital, and he's clean. So I would appreciate it if you'd drop the whole drug-thing. If he says it was these black-eyed kids, then that's exactly what it was. They were probably the ones on drugs. That would explain their dilated pupils."

The urge to stick my head out into the hallway and scream, "Damn straight!" nearly overwhelms me. Mom has my back, and that's such a relief.

"I assume Maverick has a doctor or therapist overseeing his taking of anti-depressants?" Jennings asks.

Mom replies, "Yes, of course."

"I highly recommend you make an appointment, Mrs. Ashe. This is a very difficult time for him, and he'll need professional help to get through it."

"Detective, do you think all of this might be connected to that strange cult that was reported to have set up camp on the outskirts of town? I read they recruit teenagers."

The local news had been reporting about strange activity happening around town, including freaky spray painted symbols on abandoned buildings and mutilated small animals being left in front of several churches. I never considered the cult could be responsible for killing Tarick, but it made sense.

"Like I said, I try to look at all the possibilities,"

Jennings says. "Has Maverick been socializing with new friends, kids you don't know?"

"No," Mom answers with tension in her voice. "I know all of Maverick's friends."

"Great. Thank you for your time, Mrs. Ashe. I'll be in touch."

She escorts the detective to the front door and sighs after she shuts it. Something tells me that I haven't seen the last of Detective Jennings.

THE AFTERNOON FADES and Mom finally gives up on trying to get me to eat a full dinner. The television from her room blares loud enough to seep through the walls. She won't emerge until the morning, but I'd give anything for some quiet time. Maybe my head will clear of all the nonsense going through it with some sleep.

I lay in bed, and I just can't quiet my mind. The pills the doctor prescribed for me sit on the nightstand and look more appealing by the minute. It'll help with the dull ache plaguing me and knock me out so dreams can replace the living nightmare scenes that play over and over in my head.

It takes so much effort just to swing my legs off the bed, get up, and go to my bathroom. I grab a glass, fill it with water. The round pill goes down easily with my first big gulp. I'm tempted to take my other pill, but I decide not to.

My phone buzzes again. I go to the nightstand to see who it is. Several new messages flicker on the screen. The power button is probably the best invention ever made, and it takes a few seconds to shut off. Maybe someday, I'll come up with the right words to say to Cadence, Tarick's parents, and my friends, but that day is not today.

I'm about to shove my phone in the drawer when faint taps on the window make me jump. A pair of black eyes stare back at me from outside, and the phone hits the floor right before I do.

6

ASTID

THE RAIN SLOWS to a soft drizzle, yet the humans still search. Four of them tramp through the foliage. Two dogs lead the way, going in the opposite direction from where Kren had gone. Part of me feels sorry for the people. Their search dogs will not help them.

I should leave the scene and head deeper into the woods, but I'm captivated by my surroundings. The wild animals in the area are aware of my presence and keep a safe distance from me. My movements may scatter them from their hiding places, so I have to be careful.

After several hours, panic seizes me. Kren will be furious to learn of my absence. Fi and Arion will, no doubt, try to convince him to leave me behind, but Kren will try to find me. He's determined to make me turn back to my old ways.

I vow to be in control of my own destiny.

In another hour, Kren will be too late, though. He and the others will have to return home without me. They would never wait for anyone. That's what they tell each and every one of us when we venture out. Despite Kren's devotion to me, I know that even he will not risk being captured while looking for me. At least that's my hope.

The woods are so lush with life, but the wildlife lurking in the dark are simpler than humans. People are so fraught with emotions. The human mind fascinates me, yet it seems so alien. My mind craves knowledge, more than what observation can offer.

It had been forbidden for so long to desire such things. I've always known that if I continue to give in to my curiosity about humans, that I would eventually cross that line. Each step I take and thought in my mind reeks of betrayal.

Kren would never understand my choices. To him, my decisions are unnatural. He, along with the others, relish taking the humans' lives. He will never stop trying to force me to be like him. That's why he brought *Maverick* to me.

I can still imagine the lost look of innocence being ripped from Maverick that night. I couldn't bear to feel his terror any longer. So much sorrow. After Maverick's escape, I decided not to face Kren's fury once more. Fear mainly drove my decision, but I left mostly because I knew that I had betrayed everything we had been taught.

My mind reaches out, touching the searchers, and

then recoils and withdraws. Some of them think Maverick is to blame for the other boy's death. Stepping out from the shadows and trying to explain things to these humans isn't an option. So I remain hidden, unsure of what to do next.

"The dogs picked up nothing," one of them says to another.

The other man with dark skin, who's not in uniform, puts his hands on his hips and frowns. There is no need for me to reach out to his mind to know what he's feeling.

The man says, "Maverick Ashe doesn't fit the profile. I've met a lot of screwed up teenagers, and I know in my bones that Ashe is no killer. But I'd feel better if we found something, anything at all to corroborate his story."

"Sorry, Jennings," the uniformed man says. "Wish I could be more help. My dogs are tired, and they're not picking up Tarick Lester's scent."

"Alright, thanks for your help."

They shake hands and the officers leave.

I decide to reach out to the one named Jennings with my mind. He gets in his car, so I decide to follow him. Keeping up with his vehicle isn't difficult on the dirt and grass roads, but when he hits the black road, he speeds away.

My legs push forward toward the direction he's headed, and Jennings' mind reaches beyond my range for a moment. My soaked feet squish deep into the damp earth and make it more difficult to catch up.

A large settlement of homes comes into view and Jennings' mind appears again. His confused and indecisive thoughts about Maverick jumble together. His conflict is so profound.

His vehicle comes into view, and I bend over and heave when he stops. My chest feels as if it's on fire and I'm dizzy. My breath starts to slow once again. I enter into the woods behind the homes and watch Jennings step out of his vehicle and walk up to a house.

Maverick's house.

Jennings enters through the open door, and just before I can retrieve more from his mind, he steps beyond my range again.

The insects remain silent, and the only sound is the distant vehicles driving by. It's unwise to move closer, and my indecision isn't helping. I need to help Maverick. Jennings doesn't believe he's a killer, but the other men do.

My first thought is to somehow try to communicate with Maverick, but explaining everything to him might make matters worse. He is afraid of me, and I don't blame him. Maybe if he understood the situation, however, I could help him be less afraid. I spend the next several moments trying to figure out what to do.

At the height of my uncertainty, Jennings leaves Maverick's house. Confusion and frustration still floods Jennings' mind. He believes Maverick to be both innocent and guilty, and he's sure his superiors will blame Maverick for the other boy's death. Jennings drives away, and I grasp my new found resolve.

Once darkness prevails, I know it will be time to step out of the shadows. It's time to make things right.

7

MAVERICK

M Y HEART POUNDS, and it feels as if it will break free from my chest when I see two faces peer through my window. I nearly fall over my nightstand and bolt out of my room when I realize I recognize the two girls staring at me.

"Cadence?" I whisper as I near the open window. Lisa stands next to her. "What are you doing?"

"Why haven't you answered my texts or calls?" Cadence sounds angry, but she looks like she's ready to cry.

My tired limbs ache as I jump out onto the still wet grass. "You guys shouldn't be here. I could get in big trouble. What are you doing here?"

Cadence looks like she's about to hit me. "What do you think? My boyfriend is missing and his best friend is ignoring me. People are saying all kinds of crap, and I just need to get the truth straight from you."

I shush her and close my window. It's pretty dark outside now, and the streetlights have turned on. I'm thankful that my bedroom window faces the big back yard, and I'm sure none of the neighbors can see us.

"Oh my God! What happened to you?" Lisa puts her hands up to my face.

The lotion, or maybe it's perfume, on her wrists smells like roses.

I pretend to pull away, but I let her move in closer to examine me. "I'm fine."

"You don't look fine." Her soft voice soothes me. "You look like you've been to Hell and back. What happened?"

Lisa catches me staring at her face, but Cadence steps in and gives my shoulder a little shove. I want to tell them everything, but it's just going to make things worse. They'll think I've completely lost my mind.

"I need answers here," Cadence demands. "Where's Tarick?"

Lisa looks as if she's going to defend me, but she sides with Cadence. The two of them stand silently and wait for my reply.

Stutters and stumbles come out of my mouth, but I just can't find the right words. What should I tell them? The truth? My mind races to come up with a more believable story, but I can't think straight.

Another voice cuts through the darkness. "Is this where the party is?"

The girls squeal and scurry away from the bushes.

Marcus steps out of the darkness wearing his wise-ass smile, as usual.

"Man! You want to give us a heart attack?" I'm pissed that the loudmouth is here, as I'm sure Mom will hear his booming voice. But at the same time, he brings a sense of normalcy to my messed up world.

"Sorry," Marcus says with a shrug. "I saw these two chicks sneak around back. Couldn't help myself, man."

"Marcus, you're an ass." Cadence punches his shoulder.

I point toward the gate. "Let's take this around front."

My mother's window sits twenty feet away. She probably can't hear us while her TV is on, but if I can't keep them quiet, she's bound to catch us all out here.

We exit through the open chain link fence entrance, and I latch it back in place. Mom never locks it.

Cadence grabs my arm and swings me around. "Answers! Now! My mom said you might be involved with that weird cult. That better not be true."

I take a deep breath and hold it for a second before letting it out. I'm staring at their eager faces, but I don't know what to tell them. The story goes through my mind, the events bouncing around out of order as I'm trying to figure out what I should share with them. The cops didn't believe me, and my fear is that my friends won't either.

"You all know me. I don't know what rumors are flying around, but I *did not* hurt Tarick. And I'm sure not part of any cult. The cops are on my ass because I'm the only witness, but you have to believe me. I would never hurt my best friend."

Lisa takes hold of my hand. "Of course you'd never do anything to hurt Tarick. But we need to know what *did* happen."

Against my better judgment, I decide to tell them everything. From beginning to end. I don't leave out one detail. As I'm talking, I can't tell what Lisa, Cadence, or even Marcus are thinking. They shake their heads, but I don't know if it's because they think I'm lying to them or if my story is just too crazy for them to even believe.

My story ends with the visit from Detective Jennings today. All three of them look completely lost, and now I regret telling them the truth. I wouldn't believe me either. Five minutes must have gone by when Marcus finally opens his big mouth.

"You've gotta be kiddin' me." Marcus looks down at the grass in bewilderment. "So these two had black demon eyes?"

I turn to Cadence who has tears streaming down her face. She looks like she's just about ready to burst. I'm waiting for her to start screaming at me, but she sobs silently while keeping her arms folded tightly.

Their silence eats at me, as if pieces of my sanity slowly escape with each breath. "I wish I was lying. I wish I was making it up. I saw it with my own eyes, guys. Tarick is gone, and there was nothing I could do. I know I'd be dead too if it wasn't for that freaky girl setting me free."

"And the police didn't believe you?" Lisa asks.

"Why should they? This is some crazy-ass crap that's happened. They didn't believe one word that came out of my mouth. Even though I was tested for drugs at the hospital, they still think me and Tarick were on crack or bath salts or something, which led to something bad happening."

"So what are the police doing now?" Marcus asks.

"I don't know. My mom won't let me watch TV or anything, since I'm sure the story is all over the local news. The detective said that they're searching for Tarick, but they didn't find anything. Like I said, I took the cops straight back to the exact spot where I saw Tarick's body, and he was gone. Those black-eyed freaks moved him."

Cadence looks like she's going to faint, and she sits down in the grass. Her crying gets to me. It's all my fault.

Now I'm starting to lose it. Guilt overcomes me, and I don't care if I look like a sissy crying in front of them. My hands cover my face and I turn away. Lisa's fragrant hand rests on my shoulder, but there's nothing that can comfort me right now.

Her touch disappears, and I swivel around to see Lisa crouch down to where Cadence sits. Lisa wraps her arm around her and tries her best to console her.

Marcus looks uncomfortable as he stands dumb-founded, unsure of what to do.

"Cadence, I'm sorry. I…" I don't know what to say to ease her pain, and I know she blames me for Tarick's death.

She wipes her face with her arm. "I want to see it."

"See what?" I ask.

"I want to see the barn. I want to see where Tarick was." Her words are shaky, and she has to spit them out one at a time. "I have to see it for myself."

It's a terrible idea, but maybe it'll help her. I need some allies right now, and I'm hoping for a miracle that we find some kind of clue as to where Tarick's body is.

"Okay, you know where it is," I say. "Down the road that leads to the Tower, only you don't go all the way to the end."

"No." Cadence gets to her feet. "I want to see it now and I want *you* to take me there."

I want to take her, but it's too risky. I'm uneasy about Mom finding me missing again, but I'm more terrified of those black-eyed kids being there. "I don't think that's such a good idea. Can't we wait until tomorrow morning?"

Cadence lunges towards me and I wince. I'm sure she's going to punch me. Instead, she grabs me by my shoulders. "You owe it to me, Mav. Take me to the barn."

Marcus asks the question that's weighing on my mind. "What if the black-eyed weirdos are there?"

"There's four of us and two of them," Cadence argues. "I was raised to be a good Christian, but if they're in that barn, I will kill them."

Lisa and I exchange nervous looks, and I know I'm going to regret what I'm about to say. "I'll take you to the barn, but if the black-eyed kids are there, you have to promise me that you won't do anything stupid."

She immediately refuses with an abrupt shake of her head.

I pull away and break from her grip. "Cadence, promise me you won't go all ape crazy on them. Trust me on this one. They're *not* normal. The guy was able to really screw with my mind. Not even Tarick could defend himself with whatever power the black-eyed boy had."

I'm relieved when Lisa says, "We'll call 911 instead."

"I'm a varsity wrestler," Marcus boasts. "Don't worry, guys. If that demon-jackass is there, I will kick his ass and hand him over to the cops."

Even if we had M-16s, I know it wouldn't be enough against the black-eyed boy.

I lean towards Cadence when her face softens. "Promise. Nothing stupid, okay?"

Without saying a word, Cadence nods and allows herself to be led to Lisa's Mustang, which is parked at the end of the block. We all pile in, and I decide to take the tiny backseat with Marcus.

The ride is short and quiet. Even Marcus remains

silent, which is way out of character. I look down at the floorboard for a weapon, but I only spot a small umbrella.

"It's blocked," Lisa says as we near the entrance to the barn. The stupid gate is usually open.

I crane my neck to see. "The cops must have closed it. Just pull up and leave your headlights on."

Lisa brings her Mustang right up to the gate. She puts the car in park and kills the engine. Cadence opens her door and steps out. I'm about to yell after her, but Lisa jumps out and chases her. Marcus and I struggle to squeeze out from the back of the car, and then we sprint to catch up with the girls.

The fence isn't hard to get over, even for the girls, but it's locked with a chain and padlock. Once we're over, we walk the dirt road toward the barn. Police crime scene tape surrounds the open part of the barn with one torn end that flaps in the wind.

Using the lights from Lisa's car, I get my bearings and point to the edge of the barn. I jog to the right spot. "Tarick was right here."

The others huddle around me and stare at the damp grass. We're silent for several moments, as if we're holding a memorial for Tarick. Every once in a while, I look up and stare at the dark barn, half expecting the black-eyed boy to step out and fry our brains.

"Creepy, man," Marcus says, breaking the solemn silence.

Cadence breaks down again, and Lisa holds her

up. I can't watch her cry anymore, so I turn to the barn again. I'm drawn back inside, but I stop short of crossing the barn's rotted threshold. Marcus comes up from behind me.

"This is where you were tied up?" he asks.

Without turning around, I reply, "Yeah. Right in there, under that sink." I push forward through the open police tape. A cold shiver travels up my neck when a gust of wind blows.

Marcus follows me in, but we only take three or four steps inside. Eventually, Lisa and Cadence join us. We stand in silence for a few minutes. The girls stay close together, and it feels like they're waiting for me to say something important. Lisa's headlights barely penetrate the thick darkness, and I can't see anything beyond the sink. Darkness veils the corners, and that makes me über nervous. I notice that Marcus has dropped into his wrestler's stance, which makes him look like he's going to take a crap.

"Are you ready to go?" I finally ask.

Lisa nods and tries to lead Cadence away, but she's hesitant to leave. The girls are the first to step outside, while Marcus and I bring up the rear. I'm reluctant to turn my back on the barn, but I just want to get out of here.

"Do you hear that?" Lisa's head turns toward the dark woods.

The alarm in her voice makes my heart stop. "Hear what?" I stop to listen, but I hear nothing.

Even in the darkness, I can see Lisa's wide eyes. "All of the bugs…stopped."

A deafening silence surrounds us. She's right. Not one cricket chirps. No mosquitoes zing by our ears. This is summertime in South Florida. This isn't right, and full-blown panic threatens to take over my body. We all stop and scan the area, but it's too dark to see anything. I wish I had one of those infrared goggles those ghost hunters use.

The air feels heavy. Something bad is about to happen.

"Let's get to the car." My senses are on overload, and I can *feel* that something is out there in the dark stalking us. We hasten our steps, and I catch a rustling of bushes behind us.

"Holy shiitake!" Marcus bumps into me when the sound of feet stepping in mud grows louder.

Just as we reach the fence, the swarm of bees invade my brain. My hands go to my ears, and their buzzing nearly brings me to my knees. The others must be feeling it, too. They're all stumbling, overcome by the droning of a billion bees filling up our heads. Marcus and I practically throw the girls over the fence, and somehow, we manage to will our muscles to climb over.

The world is still spinning when we reach Lisa's car. We all jump in. Cadence screams for her to get it started, and I'm relieved to be able to hear the engine come to life. The buzzing has already started to dissipate. Lisa backs the Mustang up so fast, we nearly go into a ditch. She throws the car into drive and slams on the gas. After just a mile, the bees are gone.

By the time we reach my house, even Marcus is quiet. I know they believe me now, just as I know a black-eyed kid was coming for us.

8

ASTID

TWO MINDS CLOSE in around Maverick's house, then a third. I was just about to start for his window when his friends came from the sidewalk.

The minds of the girls are constantly busy, and they both think about several things at once. The third mind, Marcus, is more simple with a single thought lingering.

Strong emotions swirl around the girl with tan skin...Cadence. She was connected to the boy Kren consumed. I have to concentrate to make sense of all that is going on in her mind. She is torn. The girl blames Maverick and believes he's hiding something. Part of her thinks that Maverick killed Tarick.

I sense Maverick's mind inside his room. I pity him. So much fear grips him. His friends tap on his window, and the first thought that comes to him is that Kren or I have come to kill him. It's strange seeing my face in the mind of another, like I'm looking in the dreaded mirror and seeing my reflection. I don't like how Maverick fears me.

He believes I am a monster.

Maverick jumps out of his window. While he recounts his story to the others, the emotions from the group churn like a dark storm. Confusion. Sadness. Anger. Hurt.

Cadence is upset that she could not be with Tarick during his last moments. I want to turn and run, never to look back on this scene again. The sensations hit me so intensely that I start to cry. Is this what it's like to be human?

When Maverick finishes telling them about Tarick, I'm thankful—and drained. I want to collapse here on the dirt and sleep, but I shouldn't. They want to go back to the barn.

As they argue among themselves, I decide to leave and head towards the abandoned farm. Maybe I can confront them there and help Maverick understand what happened to his friend.

The bare woods smell of wet dirt, and Kren isn't within range. Neither are the others. They should all be heading back home by now. I know Kren will be angry. A part of me still wonders if he will abandon common sense and stay to search for me.

Maverick and his friends arrive moments after me. Cadence especially needs to see the place where

Maverick found Tarick's body. However, she hopes to find him alive.

Memories of that night haunt Maverick. The image of his dead friend plays over in his mind. I want to scream at them to leave. There's nothing here for them. They will not find Tarick.

Even in the dark, they are as clear to me as if they were standing in front of me. My eyes prefer darkness.

Maverick and the others move silently, but their minds continue to be a tempest of fear and despair.

Another entity enters my mind field, one with more singular thoughts and purpose. It's not human, but he's hungry. It's not Kren. This one is a stranger to me. He sees Maverick and his friends, and he moves toward them while remaining in the darkness.

My mind calls out to the stranger. *Leave them alone.*

I see him stop and turn to face me. *Astid?*

His energy is still unknown to me. *Who are you?*

I am Garn. Kren is looking for you, and he sent me to help search. Why do you remain here? It is time for you to return.

The humans' only chance is for me to warn them. My mind extends its reach, stretching out to Maverick first, and then the others next.

Astid, what are you doing? Do not warn them of my presence.

I ignore him and continue to send fear into their minds. They run out of the barn and head for the car.

I feel Garn's fury. He comes towards me with death on his mind.

I was going to share. I know you particularly like the one named Maverick. You could have had him, and I would have consumed the others.

Leave here now, I command.

The car speeds off, and I'm relieved that Maverick and his friends are safe.

If I can't feed, at least I can bring you to your brother. Kren is most concerned about your recent behavior. Your affinity for these humans sickens me.

Garn continues approaching until he is only five feet from me. He is shorter than I, but he is squarely built. His fists roll tight, and I can feel the rage simmering inside of him. I work to project calm confidence, but I feel my legs shaking.

Come with me. It would please your brother if you returned with the rest of us.

Any lingering doubt about my staying here disappears, and it's replaced with determination. *No. You tell my brother that I refuse.*

Refuse? You can't stay here. Especially if you won't feed. You will die.

Garn is not worth the time it would take to explain. *Go now.*

You don't control me. I don't care if you have royal blood in your veins. All of that no longer matters. We are equals now. If you don't come with me willingly, I will make you.

His power surges, so I reach deep and let my own body's energy flow. *You can try, Garn.*

Garn's knees bend before he leaps forward. He is fast, but I am faster. His arms reach out, but I have sidestepped out of the way. I draw back my hand and strike him in the back of the neck with the meat of my palm. He grunts and tumbles forward. While taking several steps backwards, I put my hands up in preparation for his next attack.

He swivels around, but reaches out with his mind instead. His mind force is powerful, but my defenses are too strong. I put up a mental block and deflect his intrusive reach. In frustration, he lunges at me again. This time he swings his large fist toward my face.

I parry his strike with my left forearm, but I stagger backwards from the strength of the blow. His left hand makes a grab for my neck, but I back away out of arm's reach and grab his wrist instead. My mind sends a burst of energy into his arm and jolts his body. Garn's defenses are down, and I penetrate his auric field.

His body weakens and collapses onto the ground. I let go of his wrist. I could have killed him, but I have vowed never to take another life. Even one as evil as Garn's.

You leave now while you still can.

Garn rubs his injured wrist and struggles to his feet. *You're making a big mistake, Astid. Kren will not stand for this. This is the ultimate betrayal. He will find you, and then he will kill you.*

Tell him that this is my wish. I will not spend another day in the darkness. I will spend the last of my days in the sunlight, up here on the surface. I am done. Now go before I change my mind about sparing you.

He turns and runs away. I remain still, making sure that he actually leaves. The fight has drained my energy, and I find a tree to sit under. I take deep breaths, trying to soothe my weary body.

TIME PASSES by slowly when I'm alone. This is the first time I've ever been alone for this length of time. We are always in pairs, but now I am on my own.

My body feels rested but still a little drained. I decide to seek Maverick out. His emotions beckon me, almost as powerful a feeling as the energy pull from his body. Maybe I can help him. He's not responsible for his friend's death, despite his guilty feelings, and maybe I can clear his conscience and ease his suffering.

I retrace my earlier steps and easily find Maverick's house. I sense his mother inside, sleeping. Maverick is in his room awake. I connect with him, and I'm lost in his thoughts. He paces, his mind still racing from this evening's events.

He knows I was at the barn.

As he nears his window, I creep closer. I hesitate to knock as I'm sure he will be terrified, but he must know the truth. His suffering is unbearable, and I nearly buckle under the weight of his anguish.

I raise my hand to the glass and hold my breath, but before I can tap on the window, another presence surges from behind me. I haven't been careful, having been too focused on Maverick. I turn and come face to face with the girl named Lisa.

9

MAVERICK

I NEVER UNDERSTOOD why adults paced until now. My footsteps are soft, but rapid. My mind feels like it's racing a billion miles an hour, and the pacing helps me keep from losing it.

One of those black-eyed kids was there at the barn, I'm sure of it. Was it the evil boy one, or the girl that let me go? Before I can explore that thought, frantic knocking at my window startles me again.

There's no buzzing in my head, so I assume it's safe. When I reach my window, I see Lisa's fearful face on the other side of the glass. I slide my window open and she practically falls into my arms as she climbs inside.

"I saw..." she sputters as her chest heaves.

I cover her mouth with my hand in an attempt to quiet her down. Otherwise, Mom will wake up for sure. "Not so loud, okay?"

Lisa wiggles out of my grasp and shuts the

window. She locks the latch, draws the blinds, and drops to the floor with her hands above her head like she's waiting for a tornado to blow my house down.

"What is it?"

Lisa lifts her head up towards me. "I believe you."

I'm relieved that she's the first to actually admit it, but that doesn't explain the urgency on Lisa's face. She's turned pale, and she looks like she's fighting off a panic attack.

"That means a lot to me, but what is wrong with you? You look like you've seen a ghost."

"I saw her. I saw the black-eyed girl you told us about."

I feel the little hairs on the back of my neck prick up. "Where? I thought you were heading home after you dropped me off."

"She was at your window. I wanted to...well, I wanted to tell you something and decided to come to your window again, but *she* was standing there."

"Are you serious?" I check to make sure Lisa locked my window. I peer through the blinds and scan the dark yard towards the tree line. "Are you sure? I didn't hear that bee buzzing in my head, did you?"

"I did. She was here, I swear it. In the dark. I just saw the back of her while she stood near your window. At first, I thought maybe it was Cadence, even though that seems illogical to me now, since I only just dropped her off. But when I got closer, I knew it wasn't her. When I came up, the girl stared at me with her big black eyes. Scared the hell out of me. Before I could scream, she ran away. She was so fast."

"She ran off? Just like that?" I remember how she and the boy moved like lightning. It was unsettling.

Tears fall down her cheeks and she wipes them away. "I've never been more frightened in my life, Mav…never. I'll never forget those eyes."

"Maverick?" Mom yells from down the hall.

The sound of footsteps approach. There's no time for Lisa to climb back out my window, and I doubt she'd be willing to go back out there anyway. I jump up and go to the door before Mom can touch the doorknob.

"Yeah, Mom." I crack the door open. "Something wrong?"

Mom's eyes are bloodshot. "I was about to ask you the same thing. What was that noise I heard?"

"I'm okay. I just fell out of bed. Sorry."

"Nightmares?"

I nod. "I'll be fine. Go back to sleep, Mom. I'll see you in the morning."

"Alright. Goodnight." She flashes me a smile with a trace of concern and heads back to her bedroom.

I shut the door and allow myself to breathe. When I turn around to face Lisa, she's gone from her spot next to the window. She's sitting on my bed, and as terrified as I am of the black-eyed freaks waiting for us outside my window, I'm in shock that Lisa is actually in my room...on my bed. I had dreamed of this moment for years, but under much different circumstances.

"I'm sorry, Mav, but I'm too afraid to leave," she whispers.

"I know."

I sit next to her. Lisa rests her head on my shoulder, and I put my arm around her. She quivers under my touch. We sit like this for a long time until her shaking stops.

"What was she going to do, Mav? Was she coming back to kill you too?"

"I don't know."

Maybe the girl regrets letting me go, but I don't think so. Something tells me that she didn't come back to kill me. I should know better, but I can't ignore my gut feeling that she's not like the boy.

I ask her, "Are you sure she was alone? You didn't see the boy?"

Lisa shakes her head. "Just her, but that was enough." She starts to shake nervously again. "She's not human. Her black eyes make her look like a monster. And when she took off, she was a blur. But the worst was that feeling of dread. I thought I was going to die. And that loud buzzing in my head. Horrible."

"I know that feeling all too well."

That was exactly how I felt when the knocks came at Tarick's door. Without even coming face to face with the black-eyed kid, a strange and heavy feeling that I was going to die took hold of me. Froze me with fear. I swear Tarick was somehow under the boy's control, as if the monster could mess with our minds. That's why I think the girl doesn't want to kill me. If she wanted to, I'm sure she could take over my brain and I'd be dead like Tarick.

"They really killed Tarick, didn't they?" she asks.

"Yes."

"What are they?"

"I don't know."

We sit in silence for a moment, and Lisa's head leaves my shoulder.

"Vampires?" she speculates. "That boy actually asked to come in the house, right? He didn't try to just break in or anything."

"Yes, but I don't think they're vampires." I smile, thinking of that stupid movie we all saw a couple of years ago. It was so cheesy. "They didn't sparkle."

She punches my chest. "Be serious, Mav."

"He didn't go for our throats or anything," I say. "If they wanted to kill us, why didn't they just break down the door or something? Don't vampires have super-strength?"

"Maybe they are demons," she says.

"Like from Hell?" I can't help but chuckle. I stifle a louder laugh. "Demons. Really, Lisa?"

"Come to take your souls," she insists. "Poor Tarick."

"There's no way. Can't be."

"Why not? Demons have freaky eyes and their evil presence scares the living crap out of us."

I can tell that Lisa's not joking, so I try to look serious. "I guess I never really believed in Hell or demons. Just sounds so out there, but then again, this whole thing is pretty screwed up."

"One thing's for sure, Mav. They are *not* human."

I agree with Lisa on that one. "I thought they were just doped up druggies. But I know the boy was able to control Tarick's mind. Once Tarick opened the door, there was nothing we could do. It was like he had a spell over us. It took all I had to try to protect baby Cally. But Tarick looked like a zombie."

Lisa touches my arm, and I hope she needs me to hold her again. "Demons. I'm telling you. We need to do some research."

Although Lisa's theory sounds absurd, I still can't dismiss it so easily. Can't dismiss anything at this point. "Maybe you're right. Maybe they are evil demons. I should start going to church."

I'M NOT A DEMON! The voice in my head rattles my brain. I press my hands over my ears, and Lisa is too terrified to even scream.

10

ASTID

THE WORDS INVADED their minds before I could think twice about releasing them. Never before have I attempted to communicate with two minds at once. It wasn't as difficult as I had expected.

I immediately regret coming back to Maverick's house. Terror fills Maverick and Lisa while they're wondering if they had just imagined my voice in their heads. I'm about to start for his window, but I decide that I should remain in the shadows of the trees.

Maverick speaks out loud, but he's trying to push his thoughts out to me. I can easily sense his emotions, and I can almost hear his words. His effort surprises me. I didn't know humans were capable of telepathic thought. I don't hear his words clearly, but I can sense what he's asking. I think he's asking if I can hear him.

Yes, I can hear you. I project to both of them. I have

never before interacted with humans at this level. *And I am not a demon.*

Both of them look out of the window. Maverick lingers while Lisa remains on the bed. They are both afraid, but Lisa is absolutely terrified. Maverick's desire for the truth outweighs his fear.

His tenacity amazes me.

I can hear everything you think, I reply as I step out from the trees by the fence so he can see me. Maverick backs away from the window. *I mean you no harm.*

I should call the cops, Maverick thinks to himself.

They would not be able to find me, and they will not believe you.

Lisa also receives my projected thoughts, and her panic blocks her mind from being able to communicate directly with me. Maverick continues to try to send his words, and his ability to concentrate strengthens.

You killed Tarick! The intensity of his emotions knock me backwards. *Where is he?*

I still can't believe I'm sending thoughts back and forth like this with a mere human. *Kren killed him. I had nothing to do with his death.* I want so badly to join them inside Maverick's room, but I know that Lisa would become hysterical if I came to his window. *In the barn, I could have killed you. I let you go, remember?*

Lisa wants to wake Maverick's mother.

Tell Lisa not to get your mother. She is very tired and needs her rest.

Maverick does as instructed, and he remains at the window looking in my direction. *What do you want? Why are you here?*

I came to tell you the truth. I can feel Maverick's despair, but there's a sliver of hope in all of that darkness. *I am sorry for what happened to your friend.*

Where is Tarick? Where is his body?

This has been a mistake. I should never have come here. I can't tell him what I am. He would never accept me. The truth is too horrible. *I am sorry. I cannot help you.*

I turn and run into the woods until I am far enough away that I can no longer hear him. I should leave town before Kren finds me. I'm running blindly until I stop to find myself in the middle of the forest.

Despite being out of range, Maverick's grief lingers in my mind. It is too much to bear, and it's difficult to understand how humans can feel like this and yet maintain their sanity. It's too much. Maybe Maverick is right.

Maybe I am a monster.

11

MAVERICK

THE LIGHT SEEPS into the room and brightens the gloom with each passing moment. I begin to wonder if time moves more quickly now, or perhaps with everything that's been happening, it just feels that way.

Did Lisa stay the night with me? I bolt out of bed, thinking everything last night could have been just a dream, but no. Lisa stands at the window, looking out into the yard.

"The day is less scary, isn't it, Mav?" she asks me while still gazing at the new day. "It's impossible to be afraid when it's so bright out."

Lisa sends a text on her phone. "Cadence is just making sure I'm okay. She wants to see me ASAP."

"What about your folks?" I ask. "They're probably freaking out that you didn't come home last night."

"They think I'm at her house."

The digital clock next to my bed blinks 7:30, and I

know that Mom will be rising soon, if she's not already awake. "Let's get you home."

I throw the covers back and unlock my door. I hear the sound of Mom in the shower. I motion for Lisa to follow me, and we tiptoe out the front door.

When we leave the house, I can't help but look up and down the street for whatever may be lurking nearby. Do the black-eyed ghouls only come out at night? Maybe they avoid daylight just like vampires.

It's quiet outside this early, with only the mockingbirds greeting us. I open her car door and check the inside. "All clear."

Lisa stands in front of the open door and stares at me. Neither of us say a word, but her eyes speak volumes. It's a little awkward to think that we actually spent the night together. Although nothing happened, this is one for the history books. She kisses my cheek and climbs into the Mustang.

Her car leaves the development. Despite all the freaky stuff that happened last night, at least I now have an ally. Lisa believes me and that makes the situation so much better.

It's my only strand of hope.

"SCHOOL STARTS ON WEDNESDAY," Mom says as she tidies up the kitchen after breakfast.

She only fixes breakfast for us on the weekends,

since she's off of work. Every weekday, it's cereal. I finish scoffing down my second plateful of eggs.

"Do you think you'll be ready to go?" she asks me.

The thought never crossed my mind. When I looked at myself in the mirror this morning, I looked like a grotesque monster with a battered face, now purplish in color. No wonder Lisa kissed my cheek. She pitied me.

"I'll be fine."

That's a total lie. Facing all the other students who think I'm a killer scares the hell out of me.

"I'll go shopping for you today, then."

Mom is a saint. She knows how much I hate shopping, especially for clothes.

She asks, "Do you want anything special?"

"No. You know me."

"Yes, I know you." Her thin eyebrows form a knot as she lingers at the entrance to the kitchen.

I can tell she's worried, as usual. "What?"

"Are you going to be all right here…alone?"

"Yes." I want to scream *No! Don't leave me. They'll come back*. But I refuse to admit my fears.

Maybe I can call Lisa to come stay with me, but I think she might be more afraid of this house than I am. I can't blame her. Now I have them coming to my window in the middle of the night.

"Okay. Then I guess I'll see you a little later." She turns to leave and then stops. "Call me if you need anything. I won't go far."

I nod, and then she heads down the hallway.

LISA DOESN'T ANSWER my calls, and she doesn't return my messages. I pace up and down the hall wondering what I should do. Why is she ignoring me? I clear all of my other voice mails, not even listening to them. I delete all the texts I had received over the last couple of days too. I even go through my entire contacts and delete the people I no longer talk to. I'm done cleaning up my phone—now what?

Mom has only been gone an hour, and I'm already on the verge of a panic attack. I want to call her and ask her to come back. It's not like I need any new school clothes. I have all that stuff from last year that fits perfectly fine.

I breathe in and out and think about the last time I was alone. It's been a long time. I'm usually at Tarick's, or he's with me. The sad realization that I'm never going to see my best friend again hits me hard. I can't even imagine senior year without Tarick. This was supposed to be *our* year.

The Xbox remains unplayed, and I want to chuck it into the garbage. I don't even remember what game me and Tarick were playing at his house, but just looking at that game console reminds me of that night.

After flipping through the billion channels that show absolutely nothing of interest, I glare at the pill bottle on the coffee table. It's not the pain I want to escape, but the anxiety that forms in my stomach. I decide to take two, hoping it will knock me out for a while.

"MAVERICK, HONEY."

Mom's voice wakes me from a deep sleep. Her hand touches my temple and I open my eyes to see her looking down at me with concerned eyes. "How are you feeling?"

I sit up on the couch and see that the sunlight is faded outside. "What time is it?"

"It's almost seven. When I got home you were sleeping, and I didn't want to wake you." She hands me a glass of water. "Why don't you go and lie down in your bedroom for the night? Your body obviously needs the rest. And don't forget to take your Prozac."

"Okay." I take the water and make my way down to my room. Grogginess floods my brain and all I want to do is rejoin my dreams. They seem to be less scary than my reality at the moment.

Maybe I should spend the rest of my life in a coma.

MOM STILL FEELS guilty that she didn't tell me about scheduling a time for me to see a new therapist. She had woken me up to tell me that I've got an appointment first thing in the morning. I didn't put up much of a fight since I was too tired to argue with her.

We sit in her car, just outside the doctor's office.

"Maverick, I'm sorry. I should have told you last night, but you were so sleepy."

"What about Dr. Harris?"

"He retired. Very suddenly, actually. All of his patients have been referred to his replacement. Maverick, anyone who experiences what you went through needs someone, a professional, to help you sort things out. Besides, I spoke with your father about it, and he agrees. We just want what's best for you."

"Okay."

Hell, there's got to be merit in something my parents actually agree on. There is no point in arguing now. I don't have the energy to talk my way out of it, and it's not like she'll change her mind anyway. I figure if I'm not cooperative with the new therapist, they'll get the point.

"I'll see you this evening after work. Dr. Wilson's office is in 2A, on the second floor, the same as Dr. Harris.'"

Second floor? I'm exhausted just thinking about taking the steps. "Okay. Bye."

"I love you."

"I love you, too, Mom."

The glass door in front of the building slides open, and cool air hits me in the face. I take the stairs two at a time and head toward the office.

The waiting room consists of a red velvet chair next to a stack of new magazines sitting on a brown coffee table. Only one sign hangs on the door: *Dr. Tara Wilson*. She greets me as soon as I enter her office, so I must be her first patient for the day.

She's young, probably in her late twenties, which is a shock. I was expecting some old hag. A clip pulls her brunette hair back snugly and her glasses make her look super-smart and serious. No diplomas hang on the walls. As a matter of fact, the whole place lacks decoration. It's so plain and boring.

The office contains one desk, her chair, and a brown leather couch for her patients. Basically, this new shrink hadn't changed one thing from how Dr. Harris had it. And why did he retire? He couldn't have been much older than in his late fifties. I had spent three years going to see him, and I kind of miss the guy. No goodbyes, or see ya later. Makes me think we weren't that special to him after all, the little prick.

Dr. Wilson studies me. "Forgive the lack of art. I'm new in town and haven't been able to decorate yet," she says.

"It's fine." I sit on the couch and cross my arms.

She picks up a pad of paper. "Maverick Ashe. May I call you Maverick?"

"Sure." This whole thing is awkward, and I'm sure Dr. Wilson knows I don't want to be here. I hate the way she looks at me, as if I'm some kind of zoo exhibit.

"We're meeting under the worst of circumstances. Normally, I would reach out to all of Dr. Harris' patients personally. He didn't plan to retire so soon, but stated he had a family emergency and had to leave. So I apologize."

I nod. Dr. Wilson's soft voice is a nice change from Dr. Harris' usually gruff manner. Hopefully this new shrink was also quick and to the point like him too.

"So, you'll have to fill in the gaps for me. Your mother said you recently lost a friend?"

"Yes." If this shrink expects me to break down and spill my guts, she's got another thing coming.

She looks up from her notes. "Well, I'm sure that can't be easy to deal with."

"What else did my mother tell you?"

She smiles. "She said that you may have made up a story to cope with the trauma."

"Of course she did." Knowing what Mom really thinks of me feels like a stab to my chest. It hurts hearing Mom didn't believe the truth, even though she told the detective she did. I regret telling her and the cops about the black-eyed kids. No wonder they think I'm insane.

"So, you didn't make up a story?"

She's trying to paint me as psychotic, and I am determined not to fall into her trap.

"I'm not one to make up stories," I reply.

I'm not sure what hand to play here. Should I just say that I did maybe make it up because I was in shock? If I tell Dr. Wilson the truth, she will for sure start diagnosing me as crazy. I know I'm not crazy, and, now, a few friends know it too. At this very moment, I want to say Tarick ran away, but that would make me a liar.

"I'm here to listen, Maverick. I'm not here to judge, and I never will. Would you like to tell me what happened? Are you ready to talk about it?" She wheels her chair around the desk to be closer to me.

"No."

Dr. Wilson gives me a disappointed look, but I don't care.

"I'm no therapist," I say, "but isn't revisiting a traumatic event a bad thing for a crazy person to do? I thought we were going to talk about my feelings and other crap like that."

This woman looks as frigid as an ice cube. "First of all, you're not crazy. Secondly, is there something that you'd like to talk about? Your family perhaps? If you want to share what you're feeling, that's fine, too. Would that make you more comfortable? This is your time, and you're free to talk about whatever you want to share."

Ah. So every minute that ticks by is money in her wallet. *Cha-ching!*

Exhaling an extended breath, I reply, "I really didn't want to do this. I'm here to please my mom."

"I see." Dr. Wilson finally puts down her clipboard and leans forward. "I understand. Your mother is worried about you. Often times, it's difficult to be candid with people you love. People you normally trust. You're afraid that they will judge you, think you're 'crazy.' I get it."

"Yeah." I slouch back into the leather.

"Maverick, just know that whatever you say to me will not leave this room. I'm here to only listen and help you help yourself. You just have a lot of stuff on your mind, and I think I can help with that."

She smiles, and I'm pretty sure she's sincere.

"Okay. I can't help but blame myself for what happened to Tarick. I was there," I blurt out, finally relieved to say it. "I should have died too. I stood by and did nothing. Yet, I'm the one still here."

"It wasn't your fault. There was nothing you could have done about it," she tries to reassure me.

"We were playing video games when the knocks began…" I stop to look up and see that she's listening intently.

I completely ignore that little voice telling me to shut up and instead relay the entire encounter as I remember it. I start telling my story slowly, afraid she's either going to laugh or call in the guys with the straightjackets.

She remains silent, her face like stone. My words tumble out easily now, and I go into great detail describing the black-eyed kids. I tell Dr. Wilson about their weird dark eyes, the buzzing in my head, and I even tell her that these creatures had names. *Astid* and *Kren*.

I recall how I found Tarick dead, and that I was

sure the one named Kren had killed him somehow, although I didn't actually see that part since I was unconscious.

Before I realize it, an alarm clock's buzzer goes off. I jerk up from the noise, stopping my chatter.

"I'm sorry." Dr. Wilson reaches over and stops the alarm. "You can continue."

"No. That's it, really. That's how I remember it happening." I rub my knees nervously, and I decide not to talk about the next night when Marcus, Lisa, Cadence, and I went back to the barn.

"Wow. Didn't that hour go by quickly?" she asks.

I can't read her. "You think I'm nuts, don't you?"

"Maverick, far from it."

"So, you believe what I told you?" I feel both of my eyes twitch. I can't believe what I'm hearing. "You don't think I'm crazy?"

"You're not crazy," Dr. Wilson repeats. "I will say that you are hurting. You are under a lot of stress. You feel guilty. That's very normal for those who actually witness a loved one pass away."

"You have an explanation for everything I said to you this morning?" I ask her, trying to draw her into telling me what she really thinks of me. There's no way anybody can be this objective with what I just unloaded on her.

"It's not my job to explain everything. The mind is capable of doing all sorts of things to cope with trauma. All I care about is your well-being. Like I told you before we started, it's not me to judge." Dr.

Wilson glances at her notes. "And are you still taking twenty milligrams of Fluoxitine?"

"My Prozac...yeah, I am," I lie.

"Your prescription is going to expire soon, so I'm going to write you a new one." She writes something on a pad of paper before tearing off a sheet and handing it to me as I get up from the couch. "Maverick, would you like to meet me again tomorrow?"

"Why?"

"Because I think it's beneficial for you to get things off your chest, and I'm here to help you."

I shrug. I have to admit that I do feel lighter after spending time with someone who listens without interrupting me. Judging me. "Sure. Same time? I start school on Wednesday."

"Sounds great to me." She walks with me to the door. "I'll see you tomorrow, Maverick. Have a great day."

I exit her simple office, go down the steps this time, and step out into the street. Amazingly, I feel better now than when I did before entering Dr. Wilson's office. If I tell Mom that seeing a therapist was a good idea, she'll probably cry and hug me to death, but she was right after all. But instead of heading home, I decide to pay Lisa a visit. She doesn't live too far from here.

I walk down a few blocks until I get to the rich side of town. Lisa's vintage, red Mustang is parked on the street, so I know she's home. With every step I take towards the front door, my fear continues to grow until it seizes me.

She had spent the night in my room, so does that mean anything? The thought of maybe taking our friendship further terrifies me. Dr. Wilson said I'm not crazy, but I know I'm pretty messed up. Too messed up for a relationship, that's for sure.

After raising my hand to knock on the door, I stop my knuckles from rapping against the wood. How can something so innocent like knocking at the door have turned my life so upside down. I take a deep breath and gently knock anyway. The door opens, jostling me from my dark thoughts.

"Oh my God! You scared the living daylights out of me." Lisa's Mom clutches her chest. "I was walking right up to the front door when you knocked."

"Sorry. I was…"

"You can't see Lisa." She grabs onto the side of the door with one hand and closes it partially. "She's grounded, Maverick."

"Oh, I didn't know that." I put my head down and I'm somewhat relieved that I don't have to face her.

"Well, goodbye." She closes the door before I have a chance to say the same.

IT'S LATE when I return home. I had aimlessly walked around town all day, just thinking about everything. It was easy losing track of my thoughts and of time, and I don't think I managed to come to any kind of conclusion about anything. But it was better than going back to an empty house until Mom came home.

After calling Mom earlier to let her know my therapy session went okay, she said I could stay out if I wanted to, which was a surprise. I expected her to demand I go home immediately.

When I get to the house, the lights are out and I know that Mom is asleep. She goes to bed maybe just after dusk since she gets up so early.

I tiptoe through the house. Once I get to my room, I crash onto the bed. I decide not to bother with changing my clothes. The clock says that it's 8:15. It's been a long day.

I stare at the ceiling until it fades, the thoughts of the day drifting on clouds.

Maverick...Maverick...wake up.

An angelic voice echoes in my head. I hadn't fallen asleep yet, right? I had just started to, but I'm pretty sure I'm actually awake.

"What?" I grab my head with both hands.

The buzzing returns. At my bedroom window, the black-eyed Astid-girl stares at me. I fall out of bed and knock the lamp to the floor.

She's back.

12

ASTID

I'M DESPERATE. I have nowhere else to go. I'm not familiar with the area, and I don't like the idea of running into any more of Kren's lackeys.

Maverick, I need you to let me in.

I scan the woods behind me, reaching out as far as I can with my mind. I'm safe for now, but I know Kren and the others are searching for me.

I look into Maverick's room through the window, but he's hiding.

He peeks out from around his bed. *Why? So you can finish me off?*

I'm still impressed that he doesn't use his mouth to speak with me. *No, I wouldn't hurt you. If I wanted to, I could have.*

Maverick crawls closer to the window, but he averts his eyes towards the wooden floor. He's afraid to look at me. At my eyes.

And you obviously regret that, and you're here to correct that mistake. Anger invades his aura.

Maverick, please.

He finally raises his chin and stares at me. My first instinct is to take over his mind, persuade him to let me in. But that is wrong, and it's something I've vowed to never do again.

He rushes to the window. *You're hurt.*

That's when the others' energies come into my mind. They are within range. I do my best to put up my auric force field so they can't locate me, but I know they've already felt my presence. I'm hoping that by putting up my defenses, I've bought myself some time.

I distinctly felt Kren's energy before blocking them.

Yes, I'm hurt...and I'm about to get more hurt unless you let me in. I look behind me, and I can feel them closing in.

They are coming.

Maverick opens the window. "Come in. Only you."

I stumble through the opening before shutting the window closed.

As soon as I enter, I grab Maverick and push him down. I brace him against the wooden floor. A rock shatters the window. The glass cuts into my back, but I shield Maverick from the shards.

"Damn!" Maverick struggles to free himself from

under me. I rise and turn to see Avion and Garn at the window.

This isn't finished! Avion's eyes narrow. He turns to Maverick. "Let me in," he says out loud.

I grab his face and turn it towards the wall. *Don't look into his eyes, Maverick. Look away.*

"NO!" Maverick screams.

His mother calls out from her own bedroom, "Maverick?"

I back up against the bedroom door. *I will not allow you into this house, Avion, so you might as well leave.*

We will get you. Garn pulls Avion away and they disappear into the forest.

"Are you okay?" his mother yells from her bed.

I have to act fast. I exit Maverick's room and go to her door. I knock on it. Maverick follows behind me. He fears for his mother's safety, afraid I will kill her.

"I've got such a horrible headache," she says. "Come on in."

I open the door. His mother stares into my eyes and her mouth draws open.

"Don't kill her!" Maverick screams into my right ear.

My mind reaches out to his mother, and her thoughts fill with worry. So much worry. She puts her hands to her ears, and I focus my attention on easing her mind. *You're dreaming, and so very tired. I think it's best to go back to sleep.*

Maverick grabs my shoulder. "You leave her alone or I will kill you!"

"Dreaming…tired." Her worry turns into exhaustion as she closes her eyes and puts her head down on her pillow.

"Mom?" Maverick steps into her room, confused about what just happened. He touches her forehead. "Is she okay?"

She's fine. Going to sleep, that's all.

Maverick draws back his fist. "What did you do?"

Nothing. I just convinced her she was tired, and she's dreaming all of this.

The tension in his mind eases. He caresses his mother's forehead before bending over her and listening for her heartbeat. He's satisfied that she's merely sleeping, and his anger dissipates.

He follows me back to his room and glances at the shattered window. "What's going on? Who were those jackasses who busted my window?"

I close his door behind me. *They were my executioners.*

13

MAVERICK

THE WORD *EXECUTIONER* made me think of men in black hoods with axes, preparing to cut your head off. Of course, my mind isn't in the best of shape with the bees building a whole nest inside my brain. After a few short moments, they start to disappear.

A dull throb begins to threaten my head. Astid and I stare at one another for what seems like an eternity. I'm trying to figure her out, and thoughts of aliens, demons, and every scary monster I've ever read about breaches the edges of my mind.

Amazingly, I'm not so scared of her right now.

"How'd you do that?" I rub my forehead. "Make my mom decide she was tired and go to sleep."

It's easy to control the thoughts of humans, well...some of them. I'm not as strong as I was a few days ago, though.

Astid's words are crystal clear in my head despite the lingering buzzing sound.

She turns her body toward the bathroom, and I notice the blood staining the back of her sweatshirt. I'm pretty sure the flying glass cut into her, but those aren't her only injuries. When she swivels to look at me again, bruises cover her face and scrapes run up her arms and neck.

Astid smiles. *I must look ghastly.*

"That's an understatement." I regret the words as soon as they escape my mouth. "I'm sorry. I shouldn't talk. I look like somebody beat my face with a rake."

She shrugs. *It'd be best if you think your words to me rather than speaking them out loud.*

I motion toward my bathroom. This telepathy-thing is pretty creepy, but cool. *Let's get you cleaned up.*

Astid goes into the bathroom before me. I can't turn my back on her, but I'm still afraid to look at her eyes. I close the toilet seat and allow her to sit. *Can I see your back?*

She bends over. Her shredded sweatshirt looks like it has been through a grinder, and glass shards have sliced into her skin.

I mentally tell her, *Wait here. I'll be back.*

When I leave the bathroom, I decide to push my dresser over the broken window. I'm careful to avoid the glass shards on the floor. The stupid heavy thing screeches across the wood floor. I know Mom is going to wake up now.

Your mom is in a deep sleep.

Astid's words make me jump a little. Okay, so

maybe having someone in my head is more creepy than cool.

I go to Mom's room to check on her again. Her face looks peaceful, and she's breathing deeply. Maybe it's a good thing that she's able to get some decent sleep.

I run to the kitchen and gather the supplies I think I'll need. I take them back to my room and place them on the sink. Astid does an about face, and I notice the dried blood splotches on her back.

Without thinking, I begin to lift her shirt up, but then drop it back down. "Do you mind?"

No.

When I pull her sweatshirt up, a few pieces of glass fall to the floor. Her wounds aren't nearly as bad as I thought they'd be. I dab some antiseptic ointment and pick out small glass fragments with tweezers. She doesn't flinch the entire time. I know it's got to sting.

It's painful, but I'm fine.

I almost speak out loud, but I remember to think my question. *They wanted to kill you because of me, didn't they?*

Astid nods.

Because you let me go?

She nods again.

I almost feel sorry for her, but then I remind myself that it's because of the black-eyed kids that my best friend is dead. Astid might not have done it, and I'm pretty sure she's innocent. But she's one of them…whatever *them* is.

Astid turns around and pulls her shirt down. She looks up at me, and her black eyes give her otherwise normal face an otherworldly look. *I know you hate me, and yet you still help me. Why?*

I start dabbing the medicine on a cotton ball on her arms and face. It's hard to avoid staring at her eyes, but I try to concentrate on tending to her wounds instead. *I guess I couldn't let you stay out there. You looked pretty scared.*

A burning question comes to mind, and I decide to go ahead and ask it. *If you can control minds, why didn't you just force me to open the window?*

I couldn't make you let me in. I had to be allowed into your home. By choosing to open the window for me, you also open your will to me.

I shrug, as I don't really understand what she just said. A thousand more questions roam through my mind, and I wonder if she hears all of them.

What is she? Who were those two other black-eyed guys? Why do they kill us? How many are there? Will they come back?

She closes her eyes and sighs. *Maverick, I'm exhausted. I haven't slept for three days. I know you have many questions, and some of them I can't answer.*

I fight the urge to argue with her. After all I've been through, I deserve the truth. *Can't or won't?*

Both.

"There." I finish with her face. Without thinking, I ask her, "Do you want to take a shower?"

Her dirty, battered clothes cling to her body. I just can't believe I asked this black-eyed girl to hop into my shower. What is wrong with me? I have to keep reminding myself that she's not normal. Maybe they don't shower at whatever planet she's from.

I would like to, if you'd allow me.

Astid looks so pitiful right now. She might just pass out at any moment, and she's all bloody and bruised. Mom always accused me of always wanting to take care of wounded animals. I guess she's right.

I go into the room and rummage through my drawers. I hand her a t-shirt and elastic shorts that I think will fit her. She's so skinny. I turn on the shower, and I make it warm but not too hot.

Astid manages a weak grin. *Thank you.*

I close the bathroom door behind me and I decide to sit on my bed until she finishes. Am I crazy for helping this black-eyed girl like this? I feel like I'm in way over my head, but at the same time, she seems so helpless. It sounds stupid, since I know she can control my mind whenever she wants. For an instant, I panic at the thought that maybe I'm under her influence at this very second. I pinch myself, and sure enough, it hurts. I don't think I'm being controlled by her.

Astid emerges. When she walks by me, she throws me a scolding look. I have to remind myself that she can read my mind, and I'm pretty sure she knew what I was thinking while she was in the shower. Out of embarrassment, I hop off and go turn off the running water in my bathroom.

I point to my bed. *It's okay. You can rest there.*

She climbs into it. Without a word, Astid hides below the covers.

I watch her sleep from my makeshift beanbag bed across from her. Now what? My mind runs through a million different scenarios, from calling the police to somehow forcing her to answer all my questions. But I'm too tired to come to a decision.

I MUST HAVE DOZED off sometime in the middle of the night, because I wake at the sound of the front door shutting. Dread grips me, and I run out of the room to look out the front door. My mom pulls out of the driveway, and I realize she's on her way to work.

She left a note on the table:

Maverick, have some breakfast, and try to stay in today. You want to rest up for your first day of school tomorrow. Love you, Mom

I GO BACK to my room and find that Astid remains asleep in my bed. The closer I get to her pale face, the more she looks dead. Her chest isn't moving up and down and I start to freak out.

I may have a dead alien-girl in my bed.

14

MAVERICK

"ASTID? ASTID?" I shake her and put my ear to her chest, listening for her heartbeat. Nothing. I'm about to blow into her mouth when her eyes pop open. "Holy Hell." I fall on my ass next to the bed.

Maverick, is something wrong?

"I thought...you were." My breathing starts to slow. "Never mind."

You thought I was dead. Astid sits up and arches her back. She holds her side as if she's in pain.

"I was obviously wrong." I get back up and head toward the door. "Are you hungry?"

She nods.

"Do you...um, eat food like us?" It felt like a stupid question to ask, but I can't assume anything at this point.

Astid opens her mouth and says, "Yes."

I'm so used to hearing her mental words in my head, that it's shocking to hear her speak. Her voice has a musical quality to it, like it belongs to a petite choir girl.

"What do you eat?" I ask her.

She's right behind me, and I find myself hurrying down the hall toward the kitchen. It's stupid, since she slept on my bed all night. If she wanted to suck my blood, I'd be dead by now. I'm still wondering about why she wasn't breathing and why she lacked a heartbeat. Is she a vampire or something?

Fruits and vegetables.

A vegan vampire? "Do you like eggs?" I pull out the carton from the fridge.

She shakes her head. *I don't eat meat.*

Astid sits at the table, and I pull out the mixed fruit my mom likes to take to work. It's got melons, grapes, pineapple, and strawberries in it. I place it on the table and turn to get a bowl and fork. When I turn back around, she's gobbling it all up with her hands.

"Hungry?"

Very. I told you that.

Seeing her eat and hearing her thoughts at the same time sends shivers down my spine. "You haven't eaten in a while, have you?"

It has been a few days.

The phone rings and I jump. The house phone rarely rings here. I grab the cordless receiver. "Hello?"

"Mav, you're not picking up your cell phone."

It's Marcus. He never calls my home number. "I guess I forgot it in my room. Sorry."

"Man, you have trouble."

I'm not used to hearing him sound so serious, so I know this is legit. "What?" The last thing I need is more problems. "What's wrong?"

"Man, there's a black car with tinted windows watching your house. I don't think it's the cops."

I rush to the living room window and peer out. At first, everything looks normal. I look further down the street and see the dark car he's talking about. The windows are too dark for me to see who's inside.

"How long has it been there?" I ask Marcus.

"Dude, I don't know. I think it pulled up this morning when I went out to walk the dog."

Marcus isn't known for his I.Q., but I agree with him that it doesn't look like a cop car. It could be one of those unmarked ones. What if it's the CIA or FBI? Or hell, the Men in Black?

I shut the blinds. "What am I supposed to do about it?"

"What if it's the aliens, man? Maybe they came back for you. I saw on TV how aliens can make themselves look human." Marcus can't help but let me know exactly what he's thinking. "They gonna finish the job, man. You're toast. Want me to take down your last will and toaster-mint? You totally gonna leave me the Xbox, right?"

"Toaster-mint? Marcus, you're an idiot."

He gives a hearty laugh. "I've been called worse."

"I'm sure you have."

"So, whatcha gonna do?" Marcus asks.

"What am I supposed to do? If the cops are following me, so be it. I'm not surprised."

"I think we should draw him out," Marcus says.

"That's actually a pretty good idea." If it's a cop, I want him to know I'm not stupid. "Okay. I'm with you."

We're both silent on the phone until Marcus says, "Ride your bike towards my house and take the path towards town. He can't follow you in his car there."

"That means I'm going to have to go right past the black car," I say.

Marcus laughs again. "Make sure you pedal your ass off."

"Okay. And then what?"

"When he gets out of his car to follow you, I'll sneak up behind him and scare the living shiitake out of him. Pig crap. Get it…bacon…oink oink?"

Incredibly, his plan is way better than anything I had come up with. I seriously doubt it's a cop, though. It's probably a reporter or something.

"Yeah, yeah, I get it. Let's do this. Give me ten."

I hang up the phone and turn to Astid. She stares at me from the kitchen doorway with a quizzical look on her face.

"Do your people drive cars?" I ask her.

Some do. But Kren or the others are not nearby. A man is sitting in that black car you and Marcus were looking at. And he's thinking about how spying on you is such a waste of his time.

"How do you know?" I ask.

I'm reaching out and touching his mind right now.

"Is it a police officer?"

She shrugs. *I don't know. He's only thinking about having to watch you.*

"Stay in the house." I rush back to the hallway. "I'll be back soon."

I rush to my room and grab my baseball bat, but I realize how ridiculous that is. I can't hide my baseball bat while I'm on my bike. I grab my backpack off the chair and run out of the house.

What will you do? Astid mentally asks.

"That's a dumb question. You can read my mind, right?" I say out loud.

I'm in my backyard, but I've forgotten what I came out here for. Apparently I'm not good at telepathy and looking for stuff at the same time.

Yes, but if the man in the black car is with law enforcement, you will get in trouble.

"Will you stay in the house?" I'm scanning the yard and I see the shed. What I need is in there. "Don't try to stop me, okay?"

I can't go out there.

"Why?"

Because they would come for me.

I feel myself freaking out. Is some cop spying on me the least of my worries? "Are the others with black eyes out here now?"

I can't feel them, but I know they will be back.

That doesn't sound so reassuring, but I know Marcus is waiting for me. I slide the shed door open and grab the crowbar. It fits perfectly into my backpack. I swing it over my shoulder and get on my bike.

The car still sits there, and I make a point to look away from it as I pedal my bike right past him. I go right by Marcus' house towards the entrance to the development, and the car turns to follow.

This guy is pretty stupid. Even cops aren't this stupid. He's not even trying to be stealthy. I jump the curb and cruise towards the dirt path. Once the trees conceal me, I throw down my bike and hide behind a tree. I unzip my backpack and pull out my crowbar. I'm starting to believe that this whole scare tactic might be a bad idea.

I hear a car door shut, followed by the sound of rushed footsteps on the pine needles. He's running and he's coming right for me. I step out from behind the tree and raise my crowbar high in the air, and I'm staring into a barrel of a gun pointed straight at me.

15

ΛSTID

THE FURTHER MAVERICK peddles, the less able I am to hear his thoughts, which worries me. I watch the black car turn in a driveway and follow him. Maverick's emotions are all over the place, with excitement and anger being the main focus. Once he hits the woods, I lose him entirely.

I reach out to the man in the car, and I feel his frustration. He's hostile, and he wants his assignment to be over. My mind reaches deeper. He's wondering if Maverick really did survive a BEK attack. BEK... Black-Eyed Kid. That's what he calls us.

This man knows about me. He knows about us. *Maverick?*

Nothing. He cannot hear my thoughts.

I feel the presence of someone else. It's Maverick's friend. Marcus runs out of his house with a black tie wrapped around his head. He thinks all of this is a joke. He carries a wooden bat and he's excited about putting a fright into the man in the black car.

Marcus gallops towards the trees, and I can no longer touch the mind of the man following Maverick. Soon, even Marcus is out of range. I'm tempted to leave the house and go after them.

That's when I hear Maverick's voice inside my head, and the terror shoots into me so strongly, I lose my breath.

He's got a gun!

16

MAVERICK

I DROP THE crowbar and back away. I'm glad I didn't have a full bladder, because I'm pretty sure I would have wet myself when I saw the man point his pistol at my face.

"Jesus, kid!" He lowers his gun and slides it back into a holster. "Don't you know not to jump out at somebody like that? I could have shot you."

With his gun put away, my courage returns. "Who are you and why are you following me?"

I immediately study his face and examine his eyes. There's white around his brown eyes, so he's a human. Gray hair streaks his mostly black hair, and my guess is that he's maybe a little older than my own father. He looks shaken up, and I notice beads of sweat on his forehead.

"You should never have mentioned the black-eyed kids to the cops, kid. You made a big mistake and it may cost you your life."

I'm thrown off by what he just said. Did I just hear him right? "What are you talking about? How do *you* know what I told the cops?"

"I apologize." His left hand stops clutching his chest. "My name is Ronald."

"Are you a government agent or something? And what do you care about the black-eyed kids?"

I see Marcus attempting to hide behind a tree, and then he jumps to another one. Ronald turns his back to me. "Seriously, kid, give it up."

Marcus peeks out and he's got a stupid tie wrapped around his head.

I tell him, "Dude, you're an idiot."

"What's your prob, Mav? I'm trying to help you out." He holds the bat high in his hand. "So, is he a cop or something?"

Ronald turns his attention back to me. "Let's cut the crap, kid. You're of special interest to us."

"*Us*? Who is *us*? And why are you following me?"

If he's some kind of government agent, I know he could shoot me and get away with it, but I don't care. I don't like the idea of anybody watching and following me.

"Maverick Ashe, you're the one who survived a face to face encounter with a BEK, and I guarantee we are not the only people interested in that fact."

Marcus emerges from his hiding place. "Dude, you need to lighten up. So uptight and everything."

Ronald swivels around and says, "Can you leave us alone here, Rambo? We're trying to have a conversation. One that requires a few more brain cells than you currently possess," he says to Marcus.

I wave Marcus away. "It's cool. You can go home."

Marcus looks lost. "Who's Rambo?"

"Never mind." Ronald puts his hands on his hips. "Can Maverick and I have just a minute here?"

"Whatev. Catch ya later, bro." He waves at me and leaves me and Ronald alone in the woods.

I forgot about Astid. She's probably freaking out right now. I try to send her a mental message. *If you can hear me, I'm fine. I'll be back soon...I think.*

Ronald seems to know all about me, and I'm sick and tired of being in the dark. I press him further. "Who are you people? Are you a government lackey?" I look at the black sedan with dark tinted windows. "You look like a government whack-job. If you're supposed to be following me, you're doing a horrible job of being secret about it."

Ronald wags his head back and forth. "Me? No, not likely. Kid, the government are the bad guys. I'm one of the good guys, and I'm your friend, actually. I'm the only one around here who is willing to listen to you. I'm the only one who *believes* you."

"Whatever." I start toward my bike. He's not law enforcement. It's time to get home.

Ronald raises his hands, as if his open palms can block me with shear willpower. "Wait."

"Just leave me alone," I say.

Friends don't follow you around in dark cars or point guns at you. Ronald is no friend. I just want to get out of here. Away from Ronald, who apparently knows too much.

"And stop following me, or I'll call the cops."

He races to stand in front of me and places his business card into my hand. "Here. You'll want to talk to me about what happened—eventually. I may be able to help shed some light on your current circumstances and, how shall I put this, *outlook* on life in the near future."

"I doubt that." I take it and shove it into my jeans pocket.

I get on my bike and take off towards my house. If he knew my current situation, he'd piss his pants. Hey, dude, I have one at my house. I'm pretty sure I could shed some light for *you*.

"Kid, can you answer me one question?" he asks.

I ignore him, and I put more distance between me and this nut-job.

"Maverick, please. How did you get away? The BEKs never let anyone go. Never."

My whole body shivers, and all I can think to do is peddle away from Ronald as fast as I can. I risk turning my head for a second, and I see him throw his arms up in resignation and go back toward his idling car.

BEK? Black. Eyed. Kids. They never let anyone go? They'll be back for me. I know it.

My days are numbered.

17

ΛSTID

R ONALD TUNSTALL,
  Paranormal Investigator
Those are the only words on the card, above a
telephone number. I don't understand what this
means, but Maverick seems upset.

He sits in front of the coffee table and glares at it.
"I need some answers, Astid."

*I'm not sure I can answer all of your questions, Maver-
ick.* My body tenses while I sit in a chair in front of
him. I knew this moment would come. I feel like I
owe him the truth after all he's been through.

"This guy said that you never let anyone go. His
card says *paranormal investigator*. Are you guys aliens
or something? Are we being invaded?" He squints his
eyes and his mind explodes with all kinds of strange
and inaccurate possibilities.

No. We are not aliens.

There is much about my birthplace I'd rather

forget. If I had been born beyond the stars, things would be much easier. My life began surrounded by white walls and screams.

"Why can't you speak out loud? Why do you put your words into my head all the time?"

It's easier to project my thoughts and words to you, rather than try to speak your words through my mouth. Although I understand your language, it's not easy for me to communicate your way.

Maverick's frustration grows. "Why would a paranormal investigator be looking for you?"

I shudder. Ronald's mind wasn't clear to me, but I wonder if he works for those we've tried to avoid all of these years. This man seems to know some things about us. *I'm not sure.*

"What *are* you sure of?" he asks. "You're not aliens, you're not demons...what are you? Where are you from? Why do you kill us?"

His questions bring back a flood of painful memories. I'm so overwhelmed, I run to his bedroom. I shut the door and sob on the bed. The one thing I can be sure of is that I'd rather be killed by my brother or his followers than return to Level 6.

Maybe if I lure Kren and the others away, they will leave Maverick alone to live out his mortal life, but I can't be sure that Level 6 will leave him alone, either.

I may have made Maverick's life worse by letting him live.

18

MAVERICK

W ITH MY LIFE in turmoil, the last thing I need is the first day of school. I've pretty much left Astid alone since she started crying yesterday. There's something about a girl crying that makes me sick to my stomach.

Even though I dread school, I look forward to seeing Lisa and Cadence. I don't know exactly what I will tell them, but I'm hoping Astid might be more willing to open up to two girls.

Is Astid even female? Female as in the human-sense of the word. She looks like it, but I can't be sure. That's the least of my worries. How am I going to explain that I have a black-eyed girl living in my bedroom? I need answers, and Astid is the key.

I leave my room and lock the door behind me. Astid still sleeps in my bed, and I don't want Mom coming in to find her. I guess Astid could mess with her mind again, but that freaks me out. I know I've got to do something soon, and sleeping on that bean bag chair is already getting old.

"Are you all ready?" Mom asks as she sets a bowl on the table next to a box of Cheerios.

"As ready as I'll ever be," I reply in the most enthusiastic voice I can muster.

"The therapist called and said you missed the appointment yesterday."

"I completely forgot about it." I give her my puppy dog eyes as best I can. "Sorry, Mom."

"Well, Dr. Wilson said she would work with your school schedule. Can you stop by after school this afternoon to see her?"

"Aw, Mom, it's the first day of school. I don't really want to go to therapy." I want to get home to Astid as soon as possible before Mom gets back from work.

"I think it's best that you go. I'll pick you up on my way home."

She gives me a stern look that tells me that there is no way I can get out of this.

"No, I'll ride my bike home." Maybe I can cut the session short and make it home before Mom does.

"All right. Thank you, honey." She kisses my forehead. "Good luck at school today. I can't wait to hear how it goes."

She exits the kitchen, and I listen for her to start her car and drive away. I go back to my room, completely forgetting that I had locked my door.

Maybe I can leave a note, but will she be able to read it? I think she can read.

I check my watch. No time if I want to get there before the first bell rings. I would skip, but Mom would get a call from school. Who skips the first day of school anyway?

Leaving Astid here in my house alone just feels so...weird. But what else can I do? She's too afraid to be out there with the other black-eyed freaks lurking around, wanting to kill all of us.

I linger by my locked door for another few seconds before leaving the house. My bike sits on the front porch, and I'm about to get on it when a blue Corolla pulls up.

Marcus beeps the horn at me, and yells out the window, "Dude, get in."

"Since when did you get a license?" I ask as I get into his car.

"Eighth time's the charm. Just got it yesterday. You like the new wheels?"

Marcus isn't dumb. He just has a hard time focusing, which makes him a horrible driver.

I make sure to fasten my seat belt. "They actually let you pass the driver's exam?"

He pulls out and turns onto the road to school. "It wasn't easy. I had to, like, go real slow the entire time so I didn't make too many mistakes. It was the first time I didn't hit one of those darn cones. I think they just passed me so they wouldn't have to see me again.

The trick is to bug the crap out of them until they can't take it anymore."

"I think you just summed up your entire life philosophy right there." I examine the interior of the car. "Nice wheels, too. I can't believe your mom let you have the car."

"Right?"

"Marcus, man, why are you wearing the tags on your clothes?"

"It's the style, don't ya know?"

"It's only the style if you're not buying them at Walmart." I flick the generic tag hanging from his button. "And I don't think that leaving the size sticker strip down the front is considered cool."

"You wait and see. All the girls will want a piece of the Marcus Man by the end of the day."

The school looms at the top of the hill. It looks so much smaller than I remember. Buses and cars pour into the parking lot, and Marcus finds an open spot.

"So glad this is our last year." I get out and we head toward the front of school. For a second, it feels like I've forgotten something, but I quickly realize what's different. Tarick and I always rode our bikes to school together. "Thanks for the ride, Marcus."

I've been so worried about Astid in my room, I completely forgot about having to face the guys at school. They will all stare at me, pronouncing me guilty for Tarick's disappearance. At least I sort of have a few witnesses. Marcus, Cadence, and most of all Lisa. They all know I had nothing to do with it.

And all three of them know about the black-eyed kids.

"Marcus, no one can know about what happened the other night. Out in the woods."

"Shiitake, who'd believe me anyway?"

"Seriously. Let's keep this stuff between us and the girls."

"Yeah, I gotcha. Besides, I think Cadence will warm up to me soon. I mean no disrespect. Tarick was a friend of mine, too. But how long should I wait to make my move? I've had a thing for Cadence since the sixth grade."

I shake my head. "I'd lay off. She needs time to mourn."

"Like how much? A day? Give her another day?"

"Give it a little longer." Sometimes, his brain is on a different planet.

"Speak of the devils." Marcus points to Lisa and Cadence who head our way into the school's main entrance.

This is the first time I've seen Lisa since the other morning, after she spent the night with me. My mouth goes dry, and I feel my left eye twitch a little.

Lisa gives me a hug. "I'm sorry about my mom the other day."

My arms are around her shoulders, and I smell her shampoo, mixed with that yummy lotion scent. "Why'd you get grounded?"

"Because I got busted for telling them I was at Cadence's house. But don't worry, I didn't tell them anything. They'd lock me up at some psychiatric ward for sure. I'm pretty much grounded all year, which sucks."

I let go of her, even though I don't want to. "I'm sorry."

"No biggie. It's all good. I told them that I was so sleepy that I had passed out in my car after dropping Lisa off. They didn't buy it, though. Of course, my mom gave me the whole safe-sex lecture."

My face turns hot, and I'm unable to speak.

"So, what's next?" Cadence asks me.

I can tell she's pissed and that she wants to take on all the black-eyed kids on her own. "What do you mean?"

"Like, how are we going to find those monsters that killed Tarick? Should we go back to the barn with weapons? I think we need to come up with a plan of attack."

"Attack?" My gut clenches. "I don't think our weapons would be useful. I told you, they have superpowers and stuff. That black-eyed boy would snap you in half."

"We can't let them get away with this." Cadence's fingers grip the binder against her chest tighter. "No way."

"Have any of you guys told anyone else about any of this stuff?" I ask the group.

The silly grin from Marcus' face slides away. "Dude, no one would believe us. The cops already think you offed Tarick yourself, man."

I have to sometimes remind myself that Marcus lacks any kind of filter on his big mouth.

"I haven't said a word to anyone," Lisa replies. "My parents were already steaming mad at me for staying out. I couldn't get a word in edge wise through them screaming at me."

"My parents don't think I should be hanging around you," Cadence admits. "They think you had something to do with Tarick. I tried to tell them you didn't, but they believe you're a member of that cult hanging around town."

A group of kids walk by, and they stare daggers into me. So this is what the rest of my day is going to be like. Surrounded by memories of Tarick, too. Today is just going to suck.

I'm seriously thinking about being home schooled for my senior year.

Instead of staring back at everyone, I decide to look away. "It looks like parents and cops aren't the only ones who think I'm a cult-freak and murderer."

More students glare at me as they walk by.

"The girl with black eyes I saw that night. She ran off, but I know she could have killed me." Lisa grabs my chin and turns my face towards hers. "They are *real*." She turns to Cadence. "I saw the girl. She came to Maverick's window."

"What?" Cadence grabs her arm. "And you didn't tell me?"

Lisa recounts the story of the other night, and she finishes her story just before the bell rings. We are ushered into the schoolyard with everyone else. Marcus tunes out the chaos all around us and surprises me by actually listening to her the entire time.

"Dude, you didn't tell me this crap the other day when we caught that investigator guy," he says to me.

"Why am I so in the dark?" Cadence asks. "What investigator guy?"

"Meet up at lunch. We have things to discuss." I push through the bodies of other students to lead the group to the lobby.

"Hope we have the same lunch," Lisa says.

We branch off to find our homerooms in order to get our schedules. This will give me a little time to prepare. I don't know how I'm going to explain how I've got Astid at my house at this very moment. I'm hoping the rest of the day can be a distraction from all this stuff on my mind.

THE FIRST FEW classes went by fast. Luckily, I didn't have to put too much brain power into the subjects. The first day of school is pretty boring anyway. All that was on my mind was how I was going to tell Marcus, Lisa, and Cadence about Astid staying at my house. I rehearse what I will tell them, but I can't figure out a way to explain why I'm harboring a black-eyed kid.

As angry as I am about Astid's brother killing

Tarick, I know I shouldn't be angry with her, but she's keeping secrets from me. I know it. It just seems that all I'm good at doing is making her cry.

Second lunch approaches, and I know exactly where everyone will be sitting since we all pretty much hang out at the same place every year. Tarick won't be there, though. I don't know how he had managed it, but no matter where his fourth hour class was, he was always the first one at the table. He'd be sitting there with his brown bag lunch, wearing a goofy smile and waiting for all of us.

Cadence sits on the bench in the courtyard. She sees me approach, but doesn't get up. "Lisa has first lunch, damnit. How will I survive this year without her?"

That sucks. Lisa's not in any of my classes, and now she has a different lunch? Is this a cosmic conspiracy to keep us apart? With her being grounded, I'm never going to be able to see her. "And Marcus?"

She shrugs and then points. "There's the little stoner now."

"You should be nice to him. He isn't that bad."

"What ev. He just says the stupidest things sometimes."

I stare at our table for a second, imaging Tarick sitting there already. Cadence gets up, and pats my shoulder. She gives me a quick look that lets me know she's thinking about him too. I take her hand and lead her to our table.

Marcus plops down with his tray. "Man, have you seen the girls this year. It's like Victoria's Secret on steroids."

"See what I mean?" Cadence scrunches her mouth in disgust. "What you just said makes no sense."

"What?" Marcus shrugs.

"It's the same girls every year, Marcus," I say. "We've known them since elementary school."

"Yeah, but maybe this year they'll actually like me." Marcus scoots closer to Cadence. "You see my new wheels?"

"You're in my personal space, jerk." She pushes him away before taking out her lunch.

"Your eyes look messed up, man," Marcus remarks while he stares at my face. "People will think you're high on something. And the stitches on your forehead don't help."

"Look who's talking." I notice the whispers and stares crossing the courtyard. "I don't think it's my bloodshot eyes they're talking about."

"A lot of people have come up to me and asked me why I'm still talking to you," Cadence says.

"Yeah, and what did you say?" I ask.

"That you didn't do anything and I believe you're innocent." She shrugs. "I don't know what else to say. I don't want them to think I'm crazy, too."

"I get it." Everyone at school thinks I'm nuts, but at least Cadence tells them she's on my side. "It's not fun having people think you're guilty and crazy, so I do appreciate you believing me. It really means a lot."

Cadence nods, but something far away catches her attention. "Look." She points to Lisa who heads in our direction.

Lisa's without her backpack, and she's carrying a piece of paper in her hands.

"Hey guys! What's up?" Lisa takes her customary seat next to Cadence.

"You get sprung from class?" Marcus asks. "Coolio."

Lisa rolls her eyes. "No one says *Coolio* anymore, Marcus."

"It's retro," Marcus says.

"I'm taking a class break," Lisa says. "First day and all, the teachers are usually better about letting us go to the bathroom."

"I can't believe you don't have second lunch with me. What am I going to do alone with these bone-heads all year," Cadence whines.

All four of us are together, so I decide to drop the bomb on them now. "Look, guys...I have something to tell you before Lisa has to get back."

They all turn to me, as if they know what I'm about to say is important.

"The black-eyed girl that let me go..."

"The one I saw the other night?" Lisa whispers.

I nod. "She's at my house."

Cadence's mouth drops open, and her sandwich falls to the ground. Marcus stops mid-chew, and his cheeks puff out like a chipmunk's. Lisa's face turns pale white, and she shakes her head.

"You've got an alien in your house?" Marcus asks, a little too loudly. "Dude, we need to call the National Guard or something."

I now regret telling them. "No, we can't tell anyone."

"The hell we can't!" Cadence yells, and the whole courtyard full of students turns our way.

19

MAVERICK

AFTER EXPLAINING EXACTLY what happened, I managed to calm everybody down. I reminded them that Astid was the one who let me go in the first place, so I owe my life to her. It was also obvious that her brother and a couple other BEKs were after her.

Which reminded me that I still have a broken window in my room. Crap.

Lisa spent the majority of our lunch there with us, but then she had to hurry back to class. When I'm sure they rest of them have stopped freaking out, I tell them about my scheduled therapy session. Since Lisa's grounded, I need Cadence and Marcus to check up on Astid before Mom gets home from work.

"So, you promise to be nice?" I ask Cadence.

Her lips purse together and her eyebrows lean in

toward each other. I'm pushing her limits and it's written all over her face.

"I'll be cordial. I can't promise nice." She grabs her backpack from the bench. "They killed Tarick. What do you expect me to act like?"

"She didn't have anything to do with Tarick, just remember that," I say. "Marcus, you'll go with her. It's too bad Lisa is grounded."

"Yeah, man. Sure," Marcus replies.

"Oh, and just be prepared to hear her voice in your heads. It's creepy at first, but you'll get used to it. When you walk up to my house, you need to send your thoughts her way. Make sure to let her know I sent you," I say.

Marcus hears me, but I don't think he understands what I just said.

"Her name is Astid," I add.

Cadence looks like she wants to say more, but she throws away her trash and heads back to class.

Now I just have to face two more hours of school, but there's no way I'm going to be able to concentrate on whatever class rules and expectations my teachers are going to be blabbering about.

I should just skip seeing Dr. Wilson, but apparently the shrink and Mom are talking on the phone about me, and Mom has enough to deal with. So I'll go to therapy for her.

"I KNOW you're just doing this for your mom," Lisa says as she hangs a right turn towards town. "But maybe you should take your therapy seriously. You're going through a lot."

I lean my head back against the seat. "To be honest, Dr. Wilson's actually pretty good. I did feel better after our first appointment. Maybe you're right."

Lisa reaches out and touches my knee. "You're dealing with a lot at the same time. We're all pretty messed up right now. I haven't slept since Tarick died. Cadence is just angry all the time. Even Marcus isn't the same...okay, that's not true."

I put my hand on hers, and she doesn't pull away. "I'm worried about Cadence the most. She's going to blow her top. Maybe it was a bad idea to have her and Marcus go check on Astid."

"She'll be okay," Lisa assures me. "Cadence has to remember that you lost your best friend too. She's been pretty hard on you."

"I can't blame her."

"So the girl with the black eyes is named Astid," Lisa says. "They all have names?"

I nod. "She won't tell me what they are. All I know is that Astid is not a monster, demon, or an alien."

Lisa sighs. "Like I said...messed up."

I point to the building, and Lisa pulls up in front of the office building. She gives me a quick hug before I get out. Lisa drives away, and I'm tempted to ditch therapy again. I did feel better after last time, but I need to keep my secrets to myself. I sure don't plan on telling the shrink anything new this time around. If it wasn't for Mom, I wouldn't be standing here. If it gives her peace of mind, it's the least I can do for her.

Dr. Wilson's office building looms before me with not a single car in the parking lot. I wonder what she drives. Maybe she lives nearby and just hoofs it. After going up the flight of steps, I enter through the glass door and walk into the bland waiting room. I approach her office door and give it a little tap to let her know I'm here.

"One moment," her voice says from the other side of the cheap wood.

It smells like a wet basement in here. Nasty.

I wait, dreading the next hour. What am I going to say? Nothing. I'm going to say absolutely nothing. The last time I was here, I spilled my guts and told her everything. Not this time. I'm going to play it cool, and hopefully she'll tell Mom that I don't need therapy anymore. Mom will be relieved to know that her son is not insane.

Dr. Wilson finally swings the door open after a couple of minutes, and she greets me with a smile. "Maverick, it's nice to see you again."

"Hey," is all I can muster.

I stumble into the small, yet comfortable office and plop down in the same spot on the couch as last time. I resolve to make sure she knows that I'm still hurt by Tarick's disappearance, but all that stuff about the black-eyed kids was just a freaky episode I was going through. A coping mechanism or whatever they call it. Temporary insanity.

"So, how have things been since we last spoke?" She takes her seat and grabs her notebook and pen. "I'm sorry we missed each other yesterday."

"Yeah, sorry about that."

"And how are you dealing with life? Sleeping and eating okay?"

"Yep, just fine."

"And how was school today?"

Today had been rough. Anxiety filled me all day, but the worst was not having Tarick there. It was weird. I kept thinking I was going to see him at our locker after each class, and I felt my depression linger on the edge of my mind every time I had to remind myself that Tarick was gone.

"It was okay," I lie.

"How are things at home with your mother?" she asks.

I'm working hard to compose myself. "Fine. Everything's normal."

"Is there anything on your mind that you would like to talk about?"

I look into her soft, young face. She certainly doesn't look like a typical therapist. She's actually really pretty, and once again, I estimate her to only be in her early twenties. Her voice is soothing and non-threatening, but I have to remind myself to remember to be totally normal.

"No, not really," I answer her casually.

I wonder about Astid, Cadence, and Marcus. What are they doing now? Did Astid stay put all day? Will she still be there when I get home? Was she just a figment of my imagination? Maybe I am crazy and projected her into my life inadvertently.

It's so weird. It's as if I'm watching myself go through all of this crap. My life is one big out of body experience. Maybe it's stress. I need to get a grip and act normal. Dr. Wilson is looking at me, studying my every move.

Of course Astid *is* real. How will I hide her from Mom? That's the biggest question of all: what am I gonna do with Astid? I can't just keep her in hiding forever.

"You look like you've got a lot on your mind. I think we should try some relaxation techniques." Her pleasant face nods slightly and I find myself nodding as well. "It will help you feel better. It's something you can do at home when you feel a little anxious."

"Do I look anxious?" I really suck at lying. I lean back and try to look more relaxed, but judging by the discerning look on Dr. Wilson's face, she's not buying it. "I feel fine. Really."

"You look...preoccupied. Lost in your thoughts." Dr. Wilson puts down her paper and pen. "You want to try? I promise, it won't hurt. In fact, you'll enjoy it. It's just some breathing techniques, really."

"Sure." I cross my arms. I'm not so sure relaxation is the key to my problems, but I play along.

"Breathing is a good thing, I guess. I mean, if you don't breathe, you...die."

God, I sound like an idiot. I need to play it cool and just stop talking so much.

Dr. Wilson pulls out an iPod from her desk and places it in a dock connected to small speakers. "This is just some relaxing music. But I want you to focus on my voice."

"Okay."

I wonder if she heard the *I think she's nuts* tone in my voice. *Weird* describes this entire episode, and that's when I notice that all the ugly drapes completely cover the windows. The only light is coming from a small lamp on her desk. I can't believe people pay good money for this therapy-crap.

She presses play on the iPod and a soothing, light drumbeat rhythmically pulsates from the speakers. The sound of ocean waves plays in the background, accompanied by a slow playing flute. It does sound relaxing, but my mind is too full of stuff to relax. Hell, the sound of the sea rolling makes me think about the beach and how I didn't get to it nearly enough this summer. Tarick was stuck on babysitting duty to spare his folks daycare costs.

She scoots closer with her chair. "Now, lean back and try to relax, okay?" Her voice softens to almost a whisper, complementing the music echoing in the room. "We're going to begin by taking some deep breaths. I want you to inhale, hold for five seconds, and then exhale."

I do as she says. I inhale deeply, holding my breath, and finally exhaling. With my second time inhaling, I swear I smell vanilla. Now I'm a little hungry. Hold for five seconds…exhale. I uncross my arms and put my head back onto the cushion of the chair. I close my eyes, but the image of Astid's pale face and her freaky black eyes keep me from fully relaxing.

Dr. Wilson guides me through several more breathing cycles, and I'm actually feeling pretty at ease. Yeah, it's vanilla I smell for sure. Maybe I'll grab an ice cream cone on the way home.

"Now I want you to imagine that you are in a beautiful garden with lush trees and flowers all around you. There is a stone path in front of you, and you're going to take each step one at a time. And with each step, you are going to feel more and more relaxed."

Without effort, my mind constructs a pretty detailed garden. I decide to add a koi pond nearby, and I picture a large rectangular stone walkway laid out in front of me, twisting and turning all the way to the horizon. This place is gorgeous, and I'm proud of myself for imagining such a beautiful scene.

"You take your first step, and you feel the tension in your body dissolve. Take the second step, and you're feeling more relaxed, so open and easy. Third step. Your anxieties and scattered thoughts are starting to fade. If something pops into mind, let it play out and then burn away."

I mentally proceed through the path, stepping onto each old stone with purpose yet I'm feeling wonderful as I proceed through the garden. I start to actually fall asleep, and I focus on her voice to keep from going totally under. One moment, we're on step nine...and then we're on step twenty. My sense of time is a little off, and I'm wondering if I dozed.

With the sound of the music, the scene changes and I begin to imagine a pond in a beautiful wood with a waterfall in the background. Did I come up with that mental image on my own, or did Dr. Wilson suggest I imagine such a scene? I remember her saying something about creating whatever I wanted in this world, so I assume everything here is from my imagination.

The flute plays an oriental melody and I see Astid swimming in the pond beckoning me to join her. She's smiling. Even with her big black eyes, she's beautiful...more human than before.

"Maverick, you've come to the end of the path and you find yourself in the most gorgeous garden you've ever seen. Whatever it is you want, I want you to create it right there in your garden. You feel relaxed, yet aware. Do you see the pond? Hear its cascading waterfall that both relaxes and invigorates you?"

A soft voice enters my imaginary realm. "Yes." Was that me that just answered her?

"What do you see?" the voice asks.

"A wood surrounding a pond with a waterfall in

the distance." I describe the scene in my head, but I don't do the beauty justice.

The wind blows through the trees. A weeping willow hangs over the pond, and Astid swims under it.

Dr. Wilson's voice reaches from the world of reality to the world of my dreamscape. "Is there anyone there with you?"

"Yes," I reply.

Astid peeks through the willows and her eyes aren't black anymore. They are like mine, only her pupils are the color of the sea, when it's crystal clear and you can see the sand below. I can almost see into her soul.

She's perfect.

"Who is with you?"

"Astid."

I watch Astid looking at me, and, at that moment, I know, without a doubt, that she is the most beautiful girl I've ever seen. I notice every little detail of her face. She's happy I'm with her. It's as if she's talking to me without words.

"The black-eyed girl?" Dr. Wilson's voice calls out to me.

"No, she doesn't have black eyes anymore," I reply. "They are a beautiful crystal blue. She's normal now. Human."

I slowly enter the pond and wade through the water.

"What is she doing?"

"She's waiting for me." I swim closer until I cross the water and crouch in the soft sweet grass.

Astid backs under the willow, and its leaves blow across the water. I edge near the tree and part the branches. She's teasing me now, and we play a game of tag until I finally wrap my arms around her. She's so beautiful and fragile, and I want to protect her from all the bad things in this world. Our eyes lock, and I know we're going to kiss. She partly opens her lips and I move in to…

The music stops, and my willow tree vanishes.

"Maverick?"

The soothing voice vanishes; it's harsh and authoritative. Damnit. I want to go back to the dream world. I open my eyes to see Dr. Wilson. She is sitting in her chair, next to me, a profound look of worry on her young, yet professional face.

"Sorry. I must have totally fallen asleep." I blink, trying to recall the image that had just been in my mind. Crap, I was just about to kiss Astid. Astid with the blue eyes, not black anymore. It feels so far away now. Reality sucks. "Wow, how long was I out?"

"About forty minutes," she replies.

"What the hell?" I glance down at my watch and sure enough, our hour is almost up. I must have been totally out of it. I feel bad that I slept through most of our session, but hopefully Dr. Wilson will see that I'm not crazy. "I'm really sorry."

"No, that's great. It was a relaxation technique and it seemed to work well on you. I hope you are feeling better." She scoots back and her wheels squeak on the plastic mat.

I do feel more relaxed, and the tension in my shoulders is gone. I nod and take a nice deep breath. I feel pretty good.

"Now, we have a few minutes left. So, I'd like to talk about what you've been up to the last couple of days." Dr. Wilson resumes jotting down notes in her spiral notebook. "Just give me a summary of what you've been up to before school started."

"Oh, nothing really. Mom's had me cooped up at home."

Something is not right, but I can't figure out what it is. Something is off. Did I drool all over myself when I fell asleep? Maybe I snored. Dr. Wilson closes her notepad and looks at me as if she expects me to go into more detail.

I feel weird with her staring at me with this stony smile plastered on her face. Like she's a robot. What happened? I always thought she had a warm personality, and she was pretty, but she looks almost...annoyed.

My mind races to come up with something, and my moment of relaxation and being at one with the universe evaporates in a cloud of nervousness. I can't tell her that I have an alien girl living in my bedroom, but I know I can't lie to her, either. She'll see right through me. So I decide to throw her a bone.

I stand up and blurt, "Oh, and this stupid guy in a black sedan was staking out my house. A real weirdo.

At first, I thought he was a cop, but I don't know why the idiot was following me. So me and my friend put a scare in him and he drove away."

"Did he say anything to you before he left?" she asks.

Man, I need to think fast. "I think he was a reporter or something. He tried to hand me his business card, but me and my buddy pretended that we were going to beat the crap out of him with a baseball bat."

Dr. Wilson looks more than annoyed. She looks positively pissed off. And I can't shake the feeling that I'm missing something. She's about to say something when the timer dings, thank goodness.

I jump off the couch and almost sprint out of there. She follows me to the door. I just want to get out of Dr. Wilson's office. I hope this is my last session, as I have absolutely no desire to spend even just one more second with this kooky woman.

"I suggest you concentrate on your school work and forget about Ronald." She takes the clip out of her hair and it falls to her shoulders. Dr. Wilson no longer looks like a therapist, but more of an exotic dancer getting ready to transform into a sexy vixen. Now she's pretty hot. "Would you like to meet tomorrow afternoon, same time?"

Crap! She wants to meet again?

I open the door. "I'm feeling so much better now. The relaxation stuff is really great. So I don't think I need any more therapy. I'm good, thanks!"

I practically run out of her office, through the waiting room. I half-expect Dr. Wilson to run after me, but she doesn't. The midday heat has faded, and I step out into the parking lot. A sudden realization makes me feel faint. I literally almost pass out right there where I stand.

Dr. Wilson had told me to concentrate on my school work and forget about Ronald. When did I give her Ronald's name?

20

ASTID

"WE COME IN peace," Marcus says, thinking it at the same time. *We come in peace. We come in peace.*

Cadence and Marcus approach the house, and their lips move back and forth to each other. Although I can't hear what they say verbally, their thoughts ring clear. Cadence shoves Marcus into the side of the house as they near the door. They are both fearful, but anger encompasses the girl. She believes I'm responsible for Tarick's death.

I swing the door open and they both stand there staring at me with wonder. Cadence's darker skin shines in the early evening light, and her brown eyes glisten. Her hair hangs to her shoulders and she pushes one side behind her ear.

Marcus cracks a smile, flashing his white teeth. His mind fills with luscious thoughts containing both

Cadence and myself. I project just a flicker of anger at him and he takes a step back.

"We do come in peace," he whispers. "Seems you're alright. Maybe we should leave now." He grabs Cadence's arm.

"Not a chance." Cadence's resolve kicks in and her determination outweighs the fear the humans usually feel when near us.

"Come in." I use my voice to welcome them into this home that doesn't even belong to me. It feels strange opening the door and inviting them in. Such an ordinary and harmless everyday thing, yet one I've come to associate with death.

"Mav says to be nice to you, but I know you know what happened to Tarick, and you're going to tell me everything." Cadence pulls Marcus in, and his thoughts change to pure terror.

I'm doing all I can to not project my usual dark aura, which shouldn't be too difficult in my weakened state. I know Cadence's head already hurts, but Marcus doesn't seem to be as affected by my energy.

"I think my mom's calling." Marcus turns towards the street. "Let's go."

"You're not pulling that off." Cadence drags him reluctantly to the couch, and I close the door.

I don't think I can answer the questions you have, I say to them mentally.

"Holy Hell!" Marcus grabs his head as if an explosion went off inside of it.

Cadence blinks and glares at me from under her

thick eyelashes. "Mav said you can do that. Totally freaky, by the way."

It's easier for me to talk like this.

"Okay. Where's Tarick?" Cadence asks.

"Can you teach me how to do that?" Marcus asks. His thoughts move into desperate daydreams of being a superhero. "That's so awesome!"

Where's Maverick? I ask.

"Oh, he's—" Marcus begins to tell me, but then Cadence covers his mouth and shakes her head.

"First tell us about Tarick, and then we'll answer your question."

But, I read in their minds that he's at the therapist. It amazes me that even though they know I can read them, they refuse to believe it.

I can't answer your question.

Cadence doesn't really want to know the truth. She is imagining that Tarick is alive in captivity, despite what Maverick already told her. Only humans do that sort of thing. I know firsthand how humans love to keep things in cages.

Tarick is no more.

"That's all you're going to say?" Cadence asks. "I don't believe you. You're lying!"

I should never have let them in.

"I'm thinking Oprah would love to interview you. Are you up for it?" Marcus asks. Pictures of me being interviewed by a television host while he stands backstage counting money rolls through his scattered mind. There's something odd about Marcus' brain that fascinates me.

As I try to narrow in on their individual thoughts, both of their minds bombard me with so many questions, my head starts to throb. I realize now that the longer I stay here, the more people I put in danger. Why would Maverick send them here? Neither of their minds possess anything useful, and that's when something clicks inside of Cadence.

Cadence's anger boils over. She reaches out to grab my head, but I move out of the way. Her thoughts rage with images of her killing me, ripping me apart. She lunges at me once again, and all I can do is defend myself.

21

MAVERICK

"SERIOUSLY, I SENT you over here to help the situation, not worsen it." I throw my hands up in the air.

Cadence slumps in Marcus's car, and Marcus rests against the hood. I should never have sent them here. All the tension that had left my body during my therapy session has returned.

"What happened?" I ask.

"Cat fight of epic proportions," Marcus says with an impish grin. "I should've filmed it. That footage would have easily gone totally viral. It wasn't much of a fight, though. Every time Cadence went at her, the black-eyed girl just moved out of the way. She's like a ninja or something."

I'm not comforted by his sense of humor at all. I can't help but shake my head at him. "What is wrong with you, dude?"

Marcus can only shrug his shoulders.

I turn to Cadence. "I can only hope that she didn't take off. We need her. I guess I can't trust you, can I?"

She gets out of the car and folds her arms. "She knows plenty and refuses to tell us anything. I figured I'd beat the truth out of her."

"Dumbest thing I've ever heard." I glare at her. "Did it occur to you that she saved my life, and if we could gain her trust, she'd help us figure this whole thing out?"

"Maybe." A tear streams down her face. "I just want to find Tarick."

The look in her eyes tells me she doesn't believe he's dead. I can't blame her for how she feels. "I know…we just have to go about it the right way. I agree that she knows way more than she's letting on, and I promise you that I will get the truth out of her."

I poke Marcus on the shoulder. "And you, bruh, you need to rein in this craziness and focus on what we're doing. This is some serious stuff. Are we clear?"

"Yeah, man, whatever." Marcus's mouth closes into a line.

"What are we going to do now?" Cadence asks.

"I have no clue, but it's getting late and my mom will be home soon." I scan the area near my back yard. "And I'm not sure where those other black-eyed kids may be lurking. Marcus, can you take Cadence home?"

"Yeah, sure. Let's go, baby doll."

Cadence gets back into the car. "Ugh! Don't call me that, jerk."

"I think you owe Astid an apology, too," I say.

"Maybe next time." She shuts the door. After Marcus starts his car, they head down the road.

———

ASTID LAYS on my bed and stares at the ceiling. *She attacked me.*

"I'm sorry. Are you hurt?"

No. She couldn't possibly inflict pain upon me, but she wants me dead.

Her black eyes look into mine, and a shiver runs through my body. Even though she looks so alien, I almost forget she's not human. I don't need to be a mind reader to know she is shaken up. If she possesses the same kind of powers as her brother, I know she could have easily killed Cadence.

"Uh, my mom will be home soon. Did you get anything to eat today?" I look away and head toward the bean bag chair.

How was the therapist? she asks. *And I'm fine. I ate all the fruit, though, and the frozen peas.*

"Did you microwave them?" I didn't see any pans in the dishwasher or sink.

No. The peas were cold, but still edible. She sighs. *You didn't answer my question about the therapist.*

"It was fine. A little weird." I imagine her eating the frozen peas cold and scrunch my nose up. "I guess they don't have microwaves where you're from."

What does a therapist do exactly?

I shrug. That's actually a good question. "Listens to you mostly. Prescribe pills, sometimes, but mine didn't. She tried relaxation techniques on me, but the end of the session was really bizarre." I move my book bag to the side and plop down on the mushy seat. "Actually, the whole session was bizarre."

I shut my eyes and try to remember what I had dreamed about. Surely, I slept through it, but I can't recall the dream. "I told the therapist about Ronald, the guy camping outside the house in his car. I didn't tell her his name, but she somehow knew it. Maybe I mentioned it when I was out of it. I'm not sure. Dr. Wilson told me to stay away from him."

I agree with Dr. Wilson.

The front door opens and I know that I have to face my mother and her million questions about the first day of school, so I leave Astid to her thoughts… and ceiling watching.

"Just wait here, and don't make a sound. I'll grab some veggies or whatever for you after dinner, okay?"

Astid nods, but I can tell she has her doubts. She should know by now that I'm not going to call the cops on her. I close the door behind me and greet Mom in the kitchen. She puts a bag of groceries on the table and asks me how my day was.

Before I can reply, a bang echoes from my bedroom. Mom turns to me, and I feel my body break into a cold sweat. "Oh, I left my baseball bat against the wall."

I run to my room. After a deep breath, I open my door.

"What is it?" Mom asks me from down the hall.

I peek my head inside. "Astid?" The bed is empty.

In a panic, I check and see that she's not in my bathroom. My dresser is moved away from the broken window.

"My baseball bat fell on the floor. No worries," I call back to Mom. I internally kick myself for not telling her the window shattered somehow. How else will I get it fixed?

I glance out the window before moving the dresser back into place. There's no sign of Astid at all. Where did she go?

22

MAVERICK

AFTER A THOROUGH search of my entire room and then the whole house, I confirm that Astid has left her only safety net. Why was she so willing to go to her death like that? Isn't she scared that those other BEKs will find her and end her life?

Maybe she left because she feared the other BEKs will kill me.

"Mom, can I stay with Marcus tonight?"

"On a school night? Maverick, what's gotten into you?"

"Mom, I'm almost eighteen years old, I think I can manage to get to school in the morning. Besides, Marcus is driving me there now, and he lives right down the street." She's almost convinced, so I add, "It helps to be around my friends right now, that's all."

"I know, honey. And how the heck did he get a license?" She shakes her head in disbelief. "Okay, as long as you go to that therapy session, too. Dr.

Wilson says you need to talk through your problems and we scheduled another one for tomorrow."

"Okay." I know I won't be wasting my time with therapy any longer, but it's easier to get away from that discussion now and save it for another day. "Thanks, Mom." I kiss her cheek, run to my room, and stuff my school clothes into my backpack on top of my folders and paper. I also snatch up Ronald's business card, just in case.

Once I'm on my bike, I pass Marcus's house and head for the trail to town. Darkness begins to creep through the pines, and my adrenaline kicks in. There is no way I'll let Astid die to protect me. Somehow, I have to find her. I have too many questions, and I deserve to get my answers.

MARCUS ANSWERS his phone on the first ring, and I tell him, "I'm staying at your house tonight."

It's safer if I make arrangements in case Mom checks up on me. She's not a big fan of Marcus' mom, and I don't think she'll take the time to go there. If she calls Marcus, perhaps he can say I'm taking a dump or something.

"Um, okay, but I'm sleeping on the bed. You'll have to floor-it, bruh."

I exhale a frustrated breath. "I'm not *actually* staying there, Marcus."

"So, you're not staying at my house?" Marcus asks,

and pauses, confusion likely fogging his brain. "Okay, so where am I staying."

"Damnit, Marcus. You're my alibi. In case my mom calls, say I'm in the crapper." I slow my bike down.

"All right. Next time, you be the alibaba for me," Marcus says.

I actually laugh at his joke. "Sometimes, I think you act stupid on purpose."

"Don't tell anyone. It'll ruin my reputation." Marcus chuckles. "See ya." He hangs up, not even asking what it is I'm doing. I'm surprised he didn't ask about Astid either.

I ride up to Lisa's house, and her bedroom light flickers behind the blinds. I creep around the house to her window and lightly tap on it.

Luckily she's there and pulls the window open. "Maverick? You scared the living crap out of me. Seriously, you're lucky I didn't scream my head off."

"Sorry, but I need your help."

"You need my help? Why? What happened?"

"She's gone. Astid just vanished out of the house."

Lisa didn't seem sympathetic. "Cadence came by and told me what happened at your house. She's really torn up about Tarick. I'm not totally surprised she exploded like that. But, I really didn't think she'd go off the deep end."

"How did you talk to Cadence? Aren't you grounded and stuff?"

She shrugs. "My parents like Cadence. They let

her in to see me. They know all the stuff she's going through, so they made an exception."

Lisa was already on Cadence's side, and I can't blame her. But I try to convince her otherwise anyway. "Astid is very emotional, and the other BEKs are trying to kill her. I explained all that to you at lunch. I asked for Cadence's help because I was desperate. I couldn't miss another appointment with the shrink." I'm so stressed, my head starts to throb. "I can't do this alone."

"I know. I guess Cadence isn't the best person to help you at this point, though. And to tell you the truth, is it such a bad thing that Astid is gone? I mean, now you can get on with your life and we can begin to put this behind us."

If only things were that simple. "Astid's own people want her dead because she decided to not kill me. Besides, I had so many questions, but I never got the chance to ask them."

"If she was so desperate for help, why do you think she left?" Lisa asks.

I stop to think about that one before answering, "She left to protect me. Maybe she realized that coming to me put me in danger. But I need to find her. Astid has the answers I want, and I need to find out what really happened to Tarick. I won't be able to sleep until I get the truth and this town stops looking at me as if I'm a cult leader."

Lisa frowns. "I've been doing lots of research on the web about these black-eyed kids, Maverick. It's really freaky. Some people actually believe they take your soul, your human essence. It's like they're demon vampires or something, but nobody knows for sure. The BEKs come knocking on your door, and you're not supposed to let them in. It all sounds like urban legend crap, but..."

"It's all for real," I say.

She reaches out and takes my hand. "Go home and put it out of your mind. It's dark and it's late. And you don't want to be outside. You should know that better than anyone else. I'm not sure I'll ever go out after dark again. That night, seeing her...scared me to death."

"I was counting on you to be on my side," I tell her.

"I *am* on your side. But I don't think this is your fight. Let her be. She can handle her own problems." Lisa looks away. "I gotta go."

She closes her window and I'm left by myself. Lisa, always the wise one, makes a lot of sense. I should be relieved that Astid is out of my life, but I just can't let my questions go unanswered. Why doesn't Lisa want to find out more?

I pluck the card from my pocket and read it one more time: *Ronald Tunstall, paranormal investigator.* I have a feeling I'm going to regret calling him, but at this point, I don't have a choice.

EMPTY TABLES LINE THE CAFÉ, and I check the time. I have an hour left before they close it down for the night. I buy a sandwich and choose the corner booth, next to the window and as far away from the front counter as possible. I don't want anyone to recognize me talking with a strange older man.

I'm not sure what to expect from a guy who pointed a gun at me. In the back of my mind, I do want to find out what he and his so-called group know about the black-eyed kids so I can compare it to what I've learned from Astid, which isn't much. I'm curious as to how much Ronald might actually know, and maybe it'll help give me a lead in finding her.

But how much can I trust this guy?

As I take one last bite of my club sandwich, Ronald comes through the door, looks around, and spots me. His dark eyes scan the entire café one more time before coming towards me. This whole thing seems so ridiculous. He's pretending to be a secret agent, and I almost laugh out loud. Ronald stops, does an about face, and heads towards the counter to buy a coffee. What an idiot.

"Thanks for calling. I wasn't sure you would," he says as he slips into the seat opposite from me a minute later.

"Yeah, well, I had nothing better to do," I reply, trying not to sound desperate.

"Lucky me." With a silly grin, he blows on his coffee.

While I'm waiting for him to begin, because I don't know what to say, I watch him closely. His brown and gray hair recedes from his hairline and deep-set wrinkles have formed at the top of his forehead. He is probably a little older than Dad, although my father has salt and pepper hair with a tiny bit more salt these days.

There's no way this Ronald guy is involved with any government agency. He's too much of a goofball. Ronald burns his lips with his first sip of coffee, grumbling a profanity before blowing on the steaming mug once again.

I tell him, "So here I am. Although I don't know what I could possibly tell you that you don't already know." I make sure to keep my face straight when I say, "You seem pretty in-the-know to me."

Ronald looks at me questioningly, his left eyebrow arching, and he pauses before saying, "Why don't you tell me what happened that night your friend was murdered?" He stops again to take a quick swig of his coffee. "We both know Tarick was killed, don't we?"

"It's not something I really want to talk about anymore." I look down at my empty plate. Ronald's messing with me, trying to catch me off guard.

"I'm sorry if I come off a little cold," Ronald says in a low voice. "I understand what you're going through. I understand you better than anybody in the world."

I find that hard to believe, but I just shrug my shoulders instead.

"Okay." He takes yet another sip of his hot coffee, and I slurp my coke down just to annoy him. "Maverick, I've told you this before, I'm not the enemy here. The enemies are those damned beings that suck the souls out of us."

I consider playing dumb and getting Ronald agitated, but he probably knows more about the BEKs than I do. Lisa had said something about the black-eyed kids taking people's souls, so at least Ronald is being a straight-shooter with me so far.

I lean forward and decide to see just how much Ronald knows. "What do they do with our souls?"

Ronald stops and stares into my eyes for a moment before replying, "You got me, kid. There are dozens of theories. Some resemble vampire mythology. A couple of others are way out there. And I mean *way* out there. Nobody knows for sure, though. What I do know is that these BEKs *need* to kill. I think it's how they stay alive. It's like they feed off of our...essence, for lack of a better word."

So there's nothing definitive about why the black-eyed kids kill people. At the same time, what he's saying does sort of make sense and matches up with what Lisa found. My mind works fast, trying to figure out how much to reveal to him.

"Listen, I don't have the answers you want. I don't know what to say to you," I say.

He flashes me a look that he's not buying it.

I want to learn more about him and his organization, so I turn the tables on him. "Why don't you tell me how you found out about Tarick?"

Ronald looks as if he's going to take yet another drink of his coffee, but he stares into the black liquid instead. "All right. I guess fair is fair. I'll answer your questions, and you can answer mine."

"*If* I can answer your questions," I say.

I'm going to keep some stuff from him, as I'm pretty sure he will too. I wonder if this is what it's like to play poker. Just a bunch of bluffing with some truth mixed in.

"Deal." He smiles and inches forward. "There's a group of us around the world who know about the existence of these evasive creatures. Many call them black-eyed kids, or BEKs. Like I said, we have our theories, but nothing concrete…yet. The government knows about them, too, but they cover up any and all information they collect."

Okay, so Ronald and his club are a bunch of weirdo conspiracy freaks. Marcus would have a field day with this guy. I keep my mouth shut and let him continue.

"We are fortunate to have very dedicated people in my group who also happen to be in several key positions throughout the country, such as law enforcement. One of our contacts heard your story from a local police officer. You talked about kids with black eyes coming to Tarick's door. That's exactly the same story we hear from all over the world. Witness testimony comes from here in the US of A, Europe, and Asia."

My memory of that night is shoddy at best, but what Ronald says seems somewhat plausible, I guess.

Ronald grimaces when he takes another drink from his mug. "We have a network of everyday normal people who want to know the truth about these BEKs. Some are witnesses just like yourself, and that experience changes their lives forever. Usually, they become obsessed with learning about the black-eyed kids."

"Obsessed?" I push aside my plate. "Like you?"

He pauses for a long time before saying, "We all have a story, don't we, Maverick?"

Maybe this guy isn't so stupid after all. Or maybe I'm not very good at hiding my emotions, and he's reading me like a wide open book. Either way, I suddenly want to get out of here.

Ronald continues, "We *will* find out who, or what they are, and what they want with us. That's why witnesses like you are so vital. You are another piece of a very complex puzzle."

I'm no professional interrogator, but I can tell from Ronald's intense eyes and his even voice that he's leveling with me. I nod slowly, mulling over what he just revealed.

I try to imagine people all over the globe who are tracking, monitoring, and investigating all of these BEK events. It's weird, because I feel like I'm pretty much alone right now, especially since Lisa wants me to just walk away from all of this. But now, I find some comfort in knowing that there's tons of people out there who not only know about the BEKs, but who may have had an encounter.

"Your turn to answer a question," Ronald says.

I'm pretty sure I know what he's going to ask. "Fine."

"As painful as it is, I need to know what happened that night. A key part of my investigation is to gather the details of your experience and compare them to all of the testimonies we currently have."

After a deep sigh, I tell him a quick and dirty version. "A BEK in a hoodie knocked on Tarick's door while we were playing video games. Tarick opened the door, even though I told him not to. The first thing I saw was the boy's eyes. They were completely black. No pupil or any white at all. Just black. Then the kid knocked me out somehow…with just a touch of his hand. And then I awoke in that barn. I ran home after seeing Tarick's body in the grass, but the police wouldn't believe a word I said."

Ronald looks unimpressed. "That's it?"

"Yeah. I was totally out of it. I didn't see the BEK suck Tarick's soul, and I didn't see that kid again." This part was one-hundred percent true. "My friend's body was gone when I brought the police to the exact spot…"

My mouth started to quiver, and I couldn't talk anymore without the threat of totally losing it in front of Ronald overtaking me.

I'd probably kill that black-eyed demon if I ever had the chance. Kren is the BEK's name. Kren. What kind of name is *Kren* anyway?

Ronald lowers his head onto his hands. "That's so strange," was all he could muster.

"Now, my turn again. You said that many of you had encounters with the black-eyed kids, too. Like what?"

"It's extremely rare for anyone to survive an encounter, and it's impossible to prove that they were even there to begin with," Ronald replies.

He stops and squints his eyes at me. "Now, back to your story. What I meant by *strange* when you told me what happened is that you survived despite letting them into your house. That has never happened, Maverick. Witnesses often refuse to open the door because of that sudden, heavy feeling of dread when in the presence of a BEK."

Ronald really does know a lot about these black-eyed kids. A part of me wants to tell him about Astid and how she spared me, but I just can't trust him yet.

"The moment your friend opened his front door, you both were doomed. Yet, here you are." Ronald leans back and watches for my reaction.

I'm trying to formulate my response, but I'm at a loss for the right words to string together. It could just as easily have been me that Kren had taken that night.

Ronald continues, "What we do know is that these creatures look like regular teenagers, obviously, except for their black eyes. They come to people's houses or cars and always ask to be let in. They never just break in. For some unknown reason, they have to be allowed in by their victims."

"That's weird," I finally say. "Why is that? They could easily just bust their way through a door or window."

"Beats me." Ronald shrugs his shoulders. "Again, all we've got is theories. Maybe something to do with the fact that opening the door and letting them in is similar to a victim dropping his guard. Maybe allowing them in your house or car is like allowing them into your brain. I don't know. It boggles the mind."

With all of Kren's strength, why did he have to knock first? When I track down Astid, that will be one of my first questions to her.

Ronald continues, "Witnesses say that they experience an overwhelming feeling of dread right away. Not just a bad feeling. I'm talking about full on panic attack like they're going to die—even before seeing their black eyes. It's like these beings give off so much negative energy that we can sense it even from behind a closed door."

This guy is almost right on, except what he doesn't know is that after a while, that dark feeling does go away. Or maybe that's just Astid not pumping out as much negative energy. Who knows? But it sounds like no one has ever been around a BEK long enough to figure that one out, either.

"And when you let one in," Ronald says, "they have some kind of power over our minds. They can incapacitate us, much like how you were knocked unconscious. After that, it's pure speculation. Victims disappear, never to be heard from again. Except in your case."

I saw Tarick's body. I'm not sure of a lot of things about that night, but I know that it was his body out in the muddy grass. Ronald eyes me suspiciously, and I clear my throat.

I don't forget that we're trading questions, but ask another one anyway. "How do you know if it was a BEK for sure? People disappear all the time."

"We rely on our network to communicate any witness accounts of a BEK being present in the area and correlate those reported sightings with any spike in disappearances in that particular area."

"Yeah, but there's some weird cult hanging around town," I counter. "They say they recruit teenagers by kidnapping and brainwashing them."

"Of course that crossed our minds too," Ronald says. "But I was only a couple hours away, and it was convenient for me to come here and investigate anyway. After talking with you, it's clear to me that you had a real encounter with a BEK."

My heart slams against my ribs.

Ronald's face becomes grim. "There seems to be a pattern emerging when it comes to victim selection. Ninety percent of victims are young adults. Under twenty years old."

I shake the horror film image I have of Kren taking Tarick's life energy. "Why?"

"Once again, nobody knows for sure. We just have educated guesses. If they are feeding on the energy of our souls, then it would make sense that they would target younger people. Stronger, more vibrant energy."

That did make a lot of sense to me. Ronald's information sinks in, and I try to connect all the dots. Astid didn't say anything about targeting young people; then again, she didn't have time to say much at all.

"The BEKs are smart, though," Ronald says. "After they've taken a few lives, they move on. Find another location to hunt. There's no geographical rhyme or reason to their methodology. One week we'll hear of a few cases here in Florida, and next week we'll get chatter coming in from England. They seem to travel in small groups. We call them *pods*. The BEKs travel mostly in pairs, sometimes two pairs. Makes tracking them so much harder."

We're both silent for a few moments, absorbing the new revelations we've had from showing our cards. I just have to be careful not to tip my hand too much.

"Now, it's my turn." Ronald takes one final drink of his coffee and nearly spits it out. "I'm still trying to wrap my head around the reason you weren't killed." He bites his lower lip. "Sorry, I didn't mean to say it that way."

I nod, and Ronald fumbles for the right words.

"But why did the BEK put you in a barn? That makes no sense." Ronald stops and scratches his head. "I mean, I'm glad you escaped, obviously. You know what I'm getting at."

I force myself to look into his eyes and keep a steady voice as I prepare my lie. "I don't know. All I know is that when I woke up, I found myself tied up in the barn. I have no clue why he brought me there."

I stop there, replaying what I had just said, and that sinking feeling that I just messed up makes my face turn hot. I don't think I mentioned to the police about Astid freeing me from the barn either.

Hard to keep all these secrets straight.

Ronald nearly jumps out of his seat. "Tied up? How did you untie yourself?"

I slipped. I would so suck at poker. I'm such a terrible liar, and I do my best to piece my story together. "I, uh, it wasn't tied too tightly. I wiggled out of the ropes and ran out into the rain, tripped over Tarick's body. Ran home and told the cops everything that happened."

"Are you telling me the truth?" He narrows his eyes. "What is it you're not telling me, kid?"

I try to act surprised but not defensive. "Of course I am. Why would I lie? Everyone thought I was crazy after my outburst about the black-eyed kids. My mom freaked. I have to see a therapist, and I know she thinks I'm crazy, too."

"Okay." Ronald backs off, but I hope he's convinced that I'm truthful.

I don't like being in the hot seat. Ronald's asking me personal questions, so I decide to see how he likes it. "My turn. Why are *you* so interested in them?"

Ronald's mouth twists into a slight grin. Maybe he's not such a buffoon. "I see what you're getting at, Maverick." He points his finger at me.

I decide to keep pushing. "I'm spilling my guts about what happened with me, and yet I don't know anything about you. So tell me, why are you one of the dedicated watchers of the BEKs?"

"You're asking if I've had an encounter." He rubs his temples. "That's what you're getting at, isn't it?"

"Have you?" My curiosity gets the better of me and it's nice to see Ronald squirming.

"Yes. My wife. She died suddenly. Unexpectedly."

I wasn't expecting that. Ronald now has a faraway look on his face, and now I regret opening an old wound.

"But what made you think it was a black-eyed kid?" I ask.

"I just know they did it, all right?" He tilts his head to the right and left, making his neck crack. "Just know that you're not the only one who has lost a loved one to these monsters. That's why I do what I do. So that someday we will know what these BEKs are and we can make sure that no one else has to suffer."

The silence over the next few minutes is heavy,

and I'm thinking that maybe it's time to leave. But before I can even scoot my butt out of the seat, Ronald says, "Now what?"

"Now you're going to leave me alone." I sit back and match his stare.

"Kid, do you know how frustrating it is to feel so helpless? We are being hunted by real supernatural beings, and no one knows about them." Ronald's cheeks redden, and he looks pissed off. "We need to have enough hard information so that we can educate the people about this serious threat to the human race."

Ronald's pulling out the heavy dramatics to get the truth out of me. So I play the dumb teenager. "Human race? Look, man, I'm seventeen years old. School started today. I'm a senior, I think I might have a girlfriend, I'm still dealing with my parents' divorce...I've got all the normal problems on top of still dealing with the death of my best friend. And now all of this black-eyed kids stuff? I can't worry about the whole human race right now. Like I said, my mom already thinks I'm crazy."

"I'm not asking you to get in my car and help me kill these BEKs. I just want you to be totally honest with me because I've got a hunch that you're with-holding something...something important that can help me unlock this mystery."

My mouth drops open, and I'm about to lose it. Damnit I suck at lying. "I've told you everything I know. So now you leave me alone."

"You're a special case, Maverick. No one has ever reported to have had such close contact with a BEK and lived to tell about it," Ronald says, his tone almost pleading now. "There's something you're not telling me."

"I've told you the whole story," I say a little too loudly. A young couple nearby stares at us. "I bet you've somehow read the police report, right? You should know this. I told you all I know."

"Are you sure? For example, are you positive that there was only *one* BEK?" Ronald asks.

"What?" I'm so stupid. I should have just said *no*. Now he'll know I'm lying.

"They usually travel in pairs. Witnesses say there was either a pair or trio of kids. Ninety-two percent of witnesses report seeing two of them together."

I stand my ground to protect Astid. "Only one, sorry."

"Aren't you angry about what that BEK did to your friend?" Ronald asks.

"Yes, of course I am," I reply. "But there is nothing I can do about it now."

I put my trash together on the plate and rise out of my seat.

"So, that's it. You give up, just like that?" Ronald pushes my buttons, trying to get me to reveal what I've been keeping, but I know better.

"Just like that. I hope you find the black-eyed kid that killed Tarick. But I've told you all that I know. I'm sorry if it's not enough."

"You can't just walk away from this, knowing all that you do." He gets up as I move to the edge of the booth. "Please help me. Tell me everything. I've been investigating BEKs for a very long time, and a lot of what you're saying just doesn't jive with the thousands of reports we have. You're hiding something from me."

My phone chimes. I take it out of my pocket. It's a text from Lisa. *I'm sorry Maverick. I'll help you.*

I type up a reply: *You're the best. Be there soon.*

"I gotta go." I turn to leave, but Ronald grabs my arm.

"Maverick, please." A tear falls down his red cheek. "They also took my son."

23

ASTID

THE NIGHT SINGS to me. An owl hoots in the distance, the crickets call to one another, and I'm thankful to have them as my company. I feel no sign of Kren or any of the others. Regret weighs heavy on my heart, and I hope that the danger has passed for Maverick and his friends. If Kren, Avion, or Garn return to Maverick's, they will know instantly that I'm not there and begin searching elsewhere.

At least, that is my hope.

But, what if I'm mistaken? What if they decide to take their anger out on him for my desertion? They may kill him, his friends, and his mother just to cover up the knowledge that Maverick now holds. They may kill him as retribution.

I grew up hating humans. We only saw their cruelty and hate. For so long, the people at Level 6 represented the entire human race. But now, I know better. The world was also filled with people like Maverick. Good people.

Kren and his followers are the ones who are wrong.

I'm wondering if I have made a mistake. Kren and the others might come for Maverick anyway. It's not in my brother's nature to just let things go.

I turn around and head back toward Maverick's house. I need to protect him from the worst possible outcome, despite what may happen to me. It's my fault he's in danger.

It's time to stop running away.

24

MAVERICK

"WHAT THE HELL?" I stare at Ronald and wonder if he's messing with me again. But from the distress and hurt in his eyes, I know he's telling me the whole truth. "What are you telling me? That they killed your wife *and* your son?"

His mouth moves, and I think he said *They took him*, but I'm not sure. I sit back down and wait for him to explain.

"My wife was left for dead, and there was no sign of my son in the house. He just vanished." He inhales deeply, fighting back the tears that well up. "After the cops did the initial investigation, including interrogating me, they ruled him a runaway. The police searched for my son, only because he was a suspect in his mother's death until the coroner ruled she died from so-called natural causes."

I'm at a loss for words. I feel crappy for having thought that Ronald was a creep.

"After they ruled out foul play when the autopsy revealed she died of a heart condition, the authorities believed my son witnessed my wife collapse and die, and maybe ran away because of the trauma. That makes no sense at all." The struggle to keep it together overwhelms him, and he coughs instead of crying. "They didn't try real hard to look for him, since he was almost eighteen years old."

"But, what made you think it was the black-eyed kids?" I ask.

Ronald glances out the window before answering, "I put up flyers all over the place, spent countless hours searching for Ronny. He was such a good kid, and he loved baseball."

"I'm really sorry," I whisper.

"Ronny was crazy about the Atlanta Braves, and his favorite player was Chipper Jones. A co-worker of mine was able to get an autographed hat for Ronny's thirteenth birthday. He rarely took that hat off. He wore it out to the point where it was so faded and raggedy. Ronny refused to get rid of it, even though you could barely make out the signature."

The guy looks like he's on the verge of totally breaking down. So I decide to get him back on track. "So what did you do after you put up flyers?" I ask him.

"I searched everywhere for my son. One day, I'm out at the mall showing people a picture of Ronny when some guy comes up to me and hands me a folded piece of paper and walks away without saying a word."

I watch Ronald clasp his shaking hands. "What did it say?"

"It said that they knew what really happened to my family. Told me to look up *Black Eyed Kids* on the internet and call an out of state number if I wanted the truth. The message was signed, *A Friend*."

"So you went online and started reading all the stories?"

"Not at first. Eventually, I got desperate. I sat at that computer for three days straight reading all I could about the BEKs. At first, it was laughable. Then, an old lady that lived two streets away was telling her neighbors about how a couple of kids with black eyes came to her door asking if they could use her phone."

"Holy crap," is all I could muster listening to his story.

"I know. I continued to go out and put up posters of Ronny, but also asking questions about black-eyed kids. I got a lot of funny looks, and I was about to just drop the whole BEK-thing when another guy said that he had two of them bang on his car window, asking for a ride to the nearest payphone. He refused to let them in, and he took off. He didn't tell a soul, because the whole thing didn't make sense. Their black eyes really scared the hell out of him."

"I know how he feels," I say.

"And who uses a payphone these days?" Ronald

throws his hands up in the air. "Everybody and everybody's grandma has a cell phone."

I shrug my shoulders. "I don't think I've ever used a payphone in my entire life. I don't even know where they are. At the gas station maybe?"

Ronald manages a little chuckle. "And that's another strange thing about the BEKs. They might look like kids, teenagers maybe. But the way they talk, it's like they're out of the wrong era. They use outdated expressions, like asking to use a payphone."

Whoa, I hadn't thought of that. Astid does seem to be pretty out of place with modern society. I'm glad I did meet with Ronald. The man is giving me new information that I might be able to use.

"I mustered up enough courage to actually go to that old lady's house nearby, and she told me her story, too. She believed they were demons sent by the devil himself," Ronald says.

"You were then convinced the BEKs had something to do with your wife's death and your son's disappearance?" I ask.

Ronald wipes his face. "Almost. At that point, I called the number on the paper. Some guy answered and explained his network and how all of the encounters are recorded. He told me about how some of the stories get out on the internet and how many never surface. People are afraid of going public with their stories."

I am completely captivated with Ronald's tale. I feel really bad for the guy, and I'm convinced he might be able to help me get some answers. But I'm still not going to tell him about Astid. Something tells me he wouldn't show her any mercy.

"After talking with so many people who encountered these kids, I became a believer," Ronald continues. "I'm convinced my wife let them in. They took my son. There is no trace of him, and he never would have run away. This is unresolved for me. I have a dead wife and a son that disappeared in the middle of the day. I can't even begin to contemplate what happened to Ronny."

The two of us remain silent for a few minutes. We both look down at the table lost in our own thoughts. I'm reliving that night with Tarick over and over again, and the image of his body in the mud won't leave me alone.

"You and I have much in common," Ronald finally says. "We have both been victims of these creatures. One day, I will get the truth. I swear it."

I look out the window toward the dark sky. Lightning lights up the gray clouds, and I imagine thunderstorms will soon follow. Although I can't look Ronald in the face, I know that he's watching me.

"I have to go," I blurt out.

It looks like Ronald isn't going to argue. He's a man who looks defeated. "I know," he whispers.

He squeezes his hand into his pocket and pulls out his wallet. Ronald flips it open and a picture of his wife and son shows in the first plastic sleeve.

They're smiling in the photograph. His son looks like a younger version of him, but with more hair.

Ronald reaches in and retrieves another of his cards before handing it to me. "This is my number again, just in case. I'm staying at the Holiday Inn, a mile down this street. I'm in room 311. I'll be there for a while. If you're able to remember anything else, even if it seems unimportant, please either call or see me. Every little bit of information is helpful. I'd be forever grateful."

I get up from my seat. Without making eye contact with Ronald, I take his card and put it into my back pocket.

I know he's disappointed I wasn't able to give him the answers he was seeking.

Answers I'm not ready to give.

The only course of action I have consists of going back to Lisa's and hoping she has a better plan to find Astid, because I don't know where to start. Ronald was able to give me much more information on the BEKs, and maybe I've found another ally in him. But I can't be sure just yet.

He's right, though, we do have something in common. We're both emotional wrecks.

THE STREETLIGHTS around Lisa's house provide the only light. Her house is completely dark, so I assume they're all asleep. I sneak around as silently as possible while I look out for nosy neighbors. The last thing I need is for the cops to bust me for trespassing.

Someone's footsteps crunch the ground a few feet away. Adrenaline tries to block out the fear that builds up in my chest, but it's not working. I back up against the side of the house and stop. The closer the sounds come, the louder my heart thumps in my ears. A dark shadow is coming around the corner and closes in, and I'm about to pounce.

"Mav?"

It's Marcus.

"You about gave me a heart attack, dumbass." I approach him and swallow the urge to punch him in the head. "What are you doing here?"

"Lisa called me."

I'm not liking the idea of Lisa calling him. "What do you mean. She texted you?"

"No, man. She called me and said she wanted to help you find the black-eyed chick." He shoots me a wide grin. "You know, that Astid girl is pretty hot, once you look past her black eyes and mind control powers."

All I got was a text from Lisa. Why didn't she call me?

We approach her window and I tap lightly. The window rises without the lights coming on. I notice she had already taken the screen down and placed it next to the window. I don't blame her for not wanting to actually leave the house until one of us was here with her. She climbs out and hops onto the grass.

"Hey," she says to me as she smooths out the wrinkles in her pants.

"I don't want you to get in trouble with your folks," I tell her. "I'd never be able to see you again if you're caught with us."

I want to ask her why she called Marcus and not me, but I decide that this isn't the right time to act jealous.

"We need to go pick up Cadence," is all Lisa says.

"Where's your car?" I ask Marcus.

"A few blocks away. Didn't want to get noticed here."

I'm impressed he thought all of that out on his own. "Let's get going then." We head to the car. "What's the plan?" I ask Lisa.

She replies, "I don't know that I have one, but why not start from the beginning? Let's go back to the barn. We all know last time that they were near there."

"I was afraid you guys would say that." Marcus rolls his eyes. "I'll be the first to die, I bet. The stoner always bites the dust before anyone else," he says dejectedly.

25

MAVERICK

CADENCE SCROLLS THROUGH her phone. "I can't believe how many stories there are about the BEKs."

She reads yet another one to us, and we all stare at each other for several moments in silence after she's done.

"And these are just the stories that people reported," I say. "How many others have experienced similar things and kept their mouths shut?"

"This Ronald guy...do you think he's telling the truth about his son and wife?" Marcus asks. "That's messed up. I mean, losing your entire family. Soul sucking, black-eyed aliens. It's like *Invasion of the Body Snatchers* and stuff."

"He believed it, that's for sure." I remember the look in Ronald's eyes and the picture in his wallet. It all seemed pretty sincere to me.

Lisa grabs my hand and squeezes. I'm glad she

chose to ride in the back with me. "Look." She points ahead of us. Two black SUVs block the dirt road leading to the barn.

"Turn off your headlights!" I command Marcus. "Just stop for a sec."

"What's going on, dude?" Marcus asks as his headlights go dark.

Why do government agents always drive big black SUVs? I wish I had some binoculars right now. We're all staring at the cars, and there's no sign of movement. But it's too risky to try to go around them.

I reply, "Not sure, but they obviously don't want anyone going down that road. We're going to have to pull over onto the grass and park."

Marcus maneuvers his car off the road and brings it close to the woods. "What now?"

"Now, we hike," I reply. We all get out. Cadence gives me her second flashlight and we head into the woods. "Let's try to keep silent. I think we'll have to turn off the flashlights the closer we get. We don't want anyone spotting us."

"You don't think it's the BEKs?" Lisa asks. "Maybe some government agency?"

I stop to think before saying, "I think we'll be able to tell when the black-eyed kids are near. The buzzing in the head, the terror building up. I don't think the SUVs belong to them. My guess is that it's government spooks investigating the crime scene."

Marcus grabs my shoulder. "Is this such a good

idea, man? I'm not so sure we should go in the woods again. Lions and tigers and bears…oh my!"

"Shh!" Cadence slaps the back of Marcus' head. "Stop being such a pussy."

No matter how silent we try to be, our feet don't cooperate. Our footsteps make all kinds of crunching and snapping sounds, and I know that we will give ourselves away. We'd make terrible ninjas.

"Let's split up," I suggest after walking a few hundred feet. "Cadence and Marcus head that way, and circle around to the barn. Lisa and I will keep going straight. That way, we can have two points of view, and it's less likely we'll all get busted. No snitching on us if you get caught."

Cadence crosses her arms as if she's refusing to go any further. "Really? Splitting up? Isn't that a huge no no? Every horror movie where the teenagers split up never end well. Come on!"

"We're making too much noise together," I say.

Cadence looks like she wants to punch me out. "Fine, but do I have to be stuck with the damn stoner?"

"Hey!" Marcus looks sincerely hurt. "I know I'm a stoner, but I'm not a *damn* one."

I point to the path going to the left. "Just keep it down. Try to anyway."

Marcus goes first, and with a roll of her eyes, Cadence follows. I watch them until they disappear behind the trees.

I'm about to ask Lisa why she called Marcus when

she wraps herself around me and pulls my face towards hers. Her lips touch mine and I begin to relax. I place my hands behind her head and the kiss deepens. Her lips part and all the worry that was in my mind moments ago disappears. Her body presses closer to mine and I back up against a tree.

She pulls away, her eyes search my face. "I've been wanting to do that for a long time." She smiles and kisses me again.

The closeness of her body next to mine brings another urge to the surface, and I break the kiss. "How long have you wanted to do that?"

"Oh, for a few years now." She backs up and takes my hand. "Since freshman year when you were dating that bitchy blonde beach bimbo."

A quick laugh escapes my mouth. "Cassie. Girl-friend from Hell."

I didn't realize it at the time, but Cassie enjoyed guys fighting over her. She lost interest in me pretty quickly, since none of my friends fell for her charming bait. She moved on.

"What did you see in her anyway?" Lisa asks.

"Uh, she had a nice personality." Nice boobs, nice, nice butt.

"Yeah, right!" Lisa swings around, walking back-ward, and looks right into my eyes. "Well, now you're mine, and I'm not letting you go."

"Stalker!" I tease her, but I like the sound of me being hers.

"So, is it okay?" she asks.

"Okay that you're a stalker?"

"Okay, that I call you mine?"

I guess we're going to have the *relationship* talk now. Girls love that crap. "Even with my monstrous looks? You'd still want to be seen with me in public?"

She touches my still-bruised and stitched-up face. "I think your face will heal. If not, we can reevaluate the relationship at that time." She giggles.

"That's wrong on so many levels."

"So?" Lisa takes a step back, and she's waiting for my answer.

"I've wanted to go out with you since forever," I reply and bend down to give her another kiss. "If you want this to be exclusive, I'm good with that."

We wrap our arms around each other for a moment, but the sound of a bird in the dark trees remind us where we are. We try to be as silent as possible when we start through the woods once again.

As soon as we approach the barn, all the good feelings I had with Lisa quickly evaporates. I can hear voices and people moving around from somewhere just over the hill. We creep closer and hide behind a tree. I make sure to kill my flashlight.

Lisa points to the beams of light cutting through the darkness, and I scan the scene. At least twenty people surround the barn. Some have instruments that beep over the ground. I see a couple of people walking around with small video cameras. Cars litter the entire area in front of the barn, and all of the people are wearing dark suits with gloves. They poke at the grass while taking notes. Some people emerge from the barn, but I can't hear what they're saying.

I motion to Lisa to stay put. I decide to try getting closer to the barn to eavesdrop. She nods and I give her a quick kiss on the lips before I go.

I've seen soldiers in basic training do the belly crawling-thing on the ground, but it's not as easy as it looks. It's hard to move silently, so I inch slowly forward until I can find some cover behind another tree. I pop my head up to check that the coast is clear. I wonder if Cadence and Marcus got around to the back.

I'm far away enough to be hidden, yet close enough to hear these government rats' conversation.

"It's useless. They've almost certainly left," one man says to a female figure that faces away from me.

A beeper goes off, and I can't hear what the second guy says.

"Call it in," the first man says. He removes his gloves and hurries to his car. He waves his hand at the others near him and they all begin to pack up.

The woman he was talking to takes out her phone and dials. "Indications suggest they may still be in the area. Permission to stay on before we dispose of the targets."

Dispose of the targets? I hope they're talking about the BEKs. I gasp when the female agent turns her head, and the light catches her features.

It's my therapist.

26

ASTID

M Y HEAD THROBS from reaching. I can't locate Maverick anywhere. His mother remains resting in her bed, and she's almost asleep. He's not at Marcus' house, and neither is Marcus. I scan the whole neighborhood, but Maverick is gone.

Did they catch him? Does Kren have him somewhere, waiting for me to find him? If Kren did capture him, I'm sure my brother would have let me know by now. Maybe Maverick and his friends went back to the barn to try to get more answers about Tarick.

I don't have any other ideas, so I decide to go towards the barn. My defenses are up, and the only life I'm detecting are the wild animals all around me. I know I'm getting close to the barn, and I can already detect several energies just at the edge of my reach.

These minds are strangers to me, but it's still too

soon to tell. I approach cautiously, and with each step I take, I'm more certain that I'm sensing agents searching the area.

My conclusions are confirmed when I spot the two dark vehicles blocking the dirt road. I decide to go around them and stay hidden in the woods.

I start toward the barn, but then my senses become overloaded the closer I get. I slow my pace and remain at a safe distance. The human minds I'm touching tell me all that I need to know. They are searching for us, and their thoughts are full of determination and anger.

They've come for me. They know we are near, and they have weapons that will subdue us. I see them. I know them. These people are far worse than any others on this planet. Level 6 has come to take us back.

Maverick is hiding nearby. My mind is able to touch his. He's watching the agents, but he stays just out of their reach, thank goodness. Lisa is in the woods, and she's the furthest one away from the barn. I can sense Maverick crawling away on his stomach, retreating back towards Lisa's position. Marcus and Cadence, however, are getting too close.

Maverick? I send my thoughts directly to him. *Get out of there now. Do not let them see you.*

Astid? Where are you? We came here looking for you. His mental voice reaches me, and I feel him retreating from the agents' position.

I'm close by, but I need to leave here. They will kill you and do worse to me. I sense that the urgency in my words alarms him. Fear emanates from his mind.

Maverick pushes away his panic. *The others. Where are Marcus and Cadence? They should be around the barn. Can you reach them?*

My mind stretches outwards, and I dread giving Maverick bad news. *No, it's too late. They've been caught.*

27

MAVERICK

THE WIND PICKS up and crashes through the treetops. A pinecone falls nearby, and Lisa muffles a scream with both hands.

"We need to move back." I reach out and take Lisa's hand. "We're too close."

They are sending out others to look for you. You need to hurry. Astid's panicked tone penetrates my mind, and I break out into a full sprint.

Lisa remains silent and matches my pace. The pine needles and wind mask our sounds, but we stay in the wooded area, away from the road. If we continue in this general direction, we should hit the main road soon.

Where will you go? Astid asks.

I'm not sure. Talking to her in my head seems easier now. *We can't go to my house, and I'll have to get Lisa home. Marcus has the keys to his car. Who were those people? They will let Marcus and Cadence go, right?*

A million other questions pop into my head as I'm running, and they jumble together like the letters in the alphabet soup my mom likes to heat up on cold nights.

Honestly, I'm not sure what they will do to them, Astid answers. *Maverick, those people are far worse than what you imagine.*

I shudder at the thought. *One of them was my therapist.* Lisa trips over a root that sticks out of the ground, and grabs onto me for support. "Are you okay?" I ask her.

"Yeah. Where are we going?" she whispers to me as she regains her balance. "Where are Cadence and Marcus?" Her breathing becomes labored, and she grabs her chest.

I continue our frantic pace. "We can't stop. The people back there caught them."

"Oh my God, what are we going to do?" Her feet start to drag, and I'm practically yanking her across the grass. "Can we stop and figure out all this stuff?"

Astid's firm voice fills my mind. *No, you need to keep moving and beat them to the street. Cross over it and head back into the woods.*

"Oh crap, did you hear that?" Lisa asks and holds her head. "Is that...*her* in my head?"

Astid must have sent her urgent thoughts to Lisa too.

I stop to look her in the eyes. "It's Astid. She knows who those government agents are, and she's freaked out about them, so they must be bad news. Let's go, we need to get away."

Lisa starts ahead of me and kicks up dirt in her wake. It's impressive that she didn't freak out too much. Astid's mind-speak takes some getting used to —it was really weird at first—but I'm getting better at it.

A branch rakes across my arm, but panic replaces the pain. *Astid, there's a tree house a half mile from my home, in the northern woods. Will they find us there?*

No. The agents only plan to search the woods in the general area of the barn. Get there fast, she replies.

My lungs burn, but I command my body to keep moving. *Meet us at the tree house. We need answers, and it's time you give them to us.* The sternness in my thoughts remind me of my father. *Astid, I don't know what's going on, but all of this is freaking me out.*

I understand.

I mentally ask her, *Do you need directions to the tree house?*

Not necessary, Astid replies. *I know where it is from touching your mind.*

Okay, that's weird, but there's no time to dwell on that. We reach the paved road, and the sign to Bella Terra stands south of us.

"Are we going to your house?" Lisa asks.

I stop to catch my breath. "No, I don't think that's a good idea. Mom thinks I'm with Marcus, anyway."

The road appears calm, with no vehicles in sight,

and we dash across it and merge with the tree line on the other side.

"Then where are we going?"

My tennis shoes seem louder as they wade through the rougher foliage. "We're meeting Astid at the tree house just north of the development."

"We're meeting Astid? How do you know where she is? The cops can't even find her." Lisa smacks her arm. "Damnit, I'm getting eaten by giant mosquitoes."

"First of all, those weren't cops back there. They're probably something else like the CIA or FBI. Secondly, I know where Astid is because I've been using my mind to communicate with her the whole time time we've been running. I told her to meet us there."

"Talking with your mind?" Lisa quivers. "How is it I heard her once, but it seems you 'hear' her more?"

It's harder to connect to her mind, Astid says to me.

"I don't have many answers for you, yet." Talking to two women at the same time is wearing on me.

Astid, why is it that a hundred more questions pop up when you answer just one?

She replies, *Because you are a curious person, and a bit of a closed-minded one at that. I'm already at the tree house.*

"Well, I think you've opened my mind up a little here recently," I say out loud.

"What?" Lisa shoots me an annoyed look.

"Sorry, I was talking to myself." I spot the old

wooden tree house from a few hundred feet away. "Look, there it is."

A dark shadow looms at the top and moves back and forth.

"That's her, isn't it?" Lisa's voice falters. "Are you sure this is a good idea?"

"It's the only thing we can do." I turn to her to give her my best reassuring look. "I appreciate you helping me." Her hand feels sweaty within my grasp.

We approach the tree house, and I can't help but think about my childhood. My father and I spent a great deal of time building the simple wooden structure before he moved to Indiana. I shake my head loose from those thoughts. Those days are long gone.

Astid jumps to the ground with the grace of a cat leaping from a tree. Lisa squeezes my hand and jolts backward a bit. The light buzzing sound in my head grows the closer we get.

"Astid, this is Lisa. I believe you saw each other once before."

Astid nods. "Sorry…" *about scaring you.*

Lisa's unable to speak, and I wonder what she's thinking. Is Astid tuned into all of our thoughts?

Yes, I can hear all of your thoughts, she answers.

"Let's start with the obvious question," I begin. "Who were those spooks at the barn, and what will happen to Marcus and Lisa?"

The woman you thought was a therapist is one of the agents who are tracking us down and killing us if necessary. She works for Level 6. It's a secret government group who manipulated and tortured us for a very long time, until our escape.

"I'm lost...therapist?" Lisa asks.

"Yeah. Dr. Wilson was back at the barn. She just happened to take over for my old shrink after Tarick's disappearance." Some of the pieces are starting to come together, and Lisa nods in understanding. "It's obvious now that she's not a real therapist. It was all a set up."

Lisa fires away question after question towards Astid. "So, the government knows about the black-eyed kids? They've captured you before? Kind of like the aliens from Roswell or something, right?"

Level 6 created us, Astid replies with her mind.

28

ASTID

THEIR MOUTHS DRAW open. Their many questions swirl through their minds, and I'm not able to focus on any one idea or thought either are having. It's a jumbled mess.

Please, please slow your thoughts down. Focus on just one thing at a time. I can't answer everything, as I'm not sure I even know the answers myself.

"Sooo..." Lisa begins.

"What..." Maverick breaks in at the same time, and Lisa stops to allow Maverick to speak. He turns to Lisa. "Sorry."

Lisa shrugs her shoulders.

Maverick continues with his question. "What you're telling us is that the government created you and the other BEKs, and then you escaped, and now they are searching for you? So, you were created in what? A secret government lab in Area 51 or something?"

I pause to collect my own thoughts. *Yes, I was born in a lab, but the scientists always referred to the site as Level 6. My mother was the first test subject, which is why I was treated like royalty among us. However, they also took several other people from the outside world and transformed them into our kind. Those of us born this way were treated differently. We were considered pure. Up to that point, we were important to the scientists until...*

"Wait." Lisa holds her hand up and pulls on Maverick's hand. "I need to sit down."

Maverick points upward into the tree house. "We can go up there."

He helps her climb up and follows closely behind. Lisa shivers from the cool night air as she goes up the ladder. From above, Maverick looks down at me with doubt still in his eyes, and he's trying to settle his thoughts. Once they sit down on the wooden floor inside, I venture up and sit across from them. Maverick is thinking about his father building this tree house.

Maverick purses his lips together. "In the dark, it's hard to see your eyes. From here, you look like any normal person."

Lisa jabs him with an elbow. "Don't piss her off."

I see you perfectly. I'm able to see in the darkness much better than you. Maverick and Lisa exchange nervous glances. *I know this is a lot to take in, and that my appearance scares you.*

"There's just a lot we don't know," Maverick says after clearing his throat. "So what were you going to say earlier? You were important to the scientists until…what?"

Until our appetite for humans became too great. With our growing number, they couldn't feed our need for human energy fast enough. The test subjects that were created to be like us were different. They weren't as hungry as the rest of us. The scientists were also able to control them.

Maverick's fear returns, and he thinks of the man named Ronald. It seems Ronald knows a lot about us.

"Control them?" Lisa asks. "What do you mean?"

That was the objective of the entire project. The scientists wanted to create a new kind of soldier. One that not only had enhanced physical attributes, but one that could also wage psychic warfare.

Maverick lowers his face into his open hands. "That is just crazy. I can't believe they can get away with that kind of thing."

For those of us born with our abilities, they could not control us in the same way. They could only subdue us.

Lisa takes hold of Maverick's hand. "So, if the government couldn't control those of you who were born that way, did they want to just…get rid of you?"

We didn't serve a purpose for their military needs. We were an abomination, like several of their other failed experiments. We were nothing but a means to an end, and they saw us as a threat.

"Because of how you can control people's minds?" Maverick asks.

Of course. But there's something else about us they're frightened of.

Lisa scoots away from me. "And what's that?"

They are afraid of our greatest power. Everlasting life.

29

MAVERICK

S CHOOL MAY PROVIDE classes on how the government works, but it failed to teach us about all the other secret crap it does. My head aches with the overflow of new information. This was the kind of stuff you see in the movies or read in a comic book.

Lisa puts her hands over her eyes and sits in that position for a moment, and then she rubs her temples and looks up again. "I'm...I'm getting a major headache."

"So am I," I say. "I'm not sure if it's the information that I'm having trouble processing, or if it's from being next to you, Astid."

It's probably a little of both. Your minds aren't used to communicating this way, so I imagine it's taking its toll on you, Astid mentally says. *We all release an energy that helps us subdue our...prey. I'm doing all I can to keep that suppressed.*

"I'm not sure I want to hear any more about Level 6 tonight," Lisa says. "But I'm worried about Cadence and Marcus. What will happen to them?"

I wish I had the answer to that question.

Astid looks down at the floor, and I don't have to be a mind reader to know she's hiding something.

"Maybe if they feel Marcus and Cadence aren't a threat, they will let them go," I say to keep Lisa from freaking out. "I hope they keep their mouths shut." I turn to Astid. "Do you think you can hear what is going on with them?"

They are out of my range at the moment. Plus, these agents have weapons that can put even me down easily. Their biggest asset, however, is information. They know how to get the information they need. For example, the agent posing as your therapist was able to infiltrate you. I guarantee she knows more about you than you think.

My stomach does a somersault at the thought of me sitting in her office and allowing her to hypnotize me. That's exactly what those relaxation techniques were, now that I think about it. She put me under so I would tell her everything.

"She knew about Ronald, even though I hadn't mentioned his name. She probably knows about him and his group too," I say.

"That guy you talked with? The one who has the missing son?" Lisa asks.

I nod. "He's involved with a group that is researching the BEKs. But I don't think Ronald and his band of conspiracy freaks have any clue about BEKs being created in a lab or any of that stuff."

Lisa touches my face. "Mav, I really need to get home. I don't want my parents freaking out if they find me missing from my room in the middle of the night again. Plus, I really need to take something for this huge headache, and I don't even want to think about having to go to school in the morning."

"Do you think that's safe? What if Cadence and Marcus snitched on us and the agents are looking for us both?" I swivel towards Astid. "How do we get them back? I'd feel guilty for the rest of my life if my friends were taken and experimented on because they were trying to help me."

Honestly, I think Lisa would be safer at home rather than out in the open like this. Astid leans forward. *There are other things you should be even more wary about than the government agents.*

Lisa's eyes widen. "The other BEKs."

"Let's get you home then," I say. "It looks like we have more to worry about now. Astid, can you please come with us and not run away anymore? If the other BEKs are around, you would know, right?"

She nods and we climb down the ladder.

"It looks like we are hoofing it, and the trail to town is probably the safest route." I start to lead them towards the woods. "I have a feeling we need to stay away from the roads."

30

MAVERICK

IT'S BEEN TWO days. Two long days since Marcus and Cadence went missing. Despite the optimist in me thinking the government agents would just let them go, my gut tells me that something is very wrong. They wouldn't just kill a couple of innocent teenagers, would they?

If Level 6 is willing to create demon-babies in a lab, or turn kids into BEKs and control them like robots, then its capable of pretty much doing whatever it wants.

Mom also saw that my window was broken, and she just about had a heart attack. It pained me to have to lie to her again. I said that some punks threw a rock through it. I told her that they probably did it because they think I killed Tarick.

With Mom panicking about vandals attacking my room, there was no way Astid could stay with me. Astid spent one night in the tree house, but Lisa offered to sneak her into her room. That surprised the heck out of me. I know she's starting to trust Astid, but it's actually a smart move on her part. If Kren and his goons are nearby, Lisa's got her BEK alarm system with her.

School for the next two days resembles Hell. Lisa and I try to put on normal faces, but knowing what really happened to Marcus and Cadence beats us up inside.

The police continue to search for them. Just yesterday, Detective Jennings questioned me and Lisa. Astid thought it would be best if we didn't mention anything regarding Level 6 and the government agents. She's convinced it would do more harm than good. Lisa disagrees, but she later texted me and reassured me that she didn't say anything to the detective.

So I told Jennings that I spent the night at Lisa's instead of going to Marcus' house. That made him uncomfortable, but he confirmed it with Lisa too. Nothing like a tale of teenage lust to throw the bloodhound off the trail.

As Jennings turned to leave my house, he looked me straight in the eyes for a long time. I don't blame him, though. I'm pretty sure the police think I'm some kind of teen murderer or something. In fact, I kept looking out the window to see if the cops were going to be watching my house. Maybe I'm paranoid, or maybe I should start taking my meds so I don't start sinking even lower.

The cafeteria is bustling with kids. The smell of pizza sauce and tater tots fill the entire area. Maybe if I let the everyday world back into my life, things won't seem so messed up. Even the teachers look at me weird. They probably think that I'm not only a member of that religious cult kidnapping teenagers, but that I'm the its leader.

Lisa sneaks out of class just for a little bit, but she can't stay long.

"I still don't like lying to the police," she says to me.

"The cops already think I'm crazy. I was already on their radar when Tarick disappeared. If I started talking about secret agents and stuff, they'd throw me in a padded cell for sure."

Lisa frowns. She knows I'm right.

"If Level 6 learns we talked to the cops about them, we're totally screwed. They'll make us disappear. It's best that the spooks think that we don't know anything."

"But why don't they just come in here and take us away right now?" Lisa asks. "What's to stop government agents from busting through your door at night and throwing you in a black van and hauling you off to who knows where?"

I stop to think about that for a moment. "Maybe they think that tailing us can lead them to the BEKs. They want something from me. That would explain why one of those spooks pretended to be my therapist." I take a bite of my sandwich.

Lisa scoots closer to me, her hall pass in her hands. "Maverick, I'm really scared. I'm worried about Marcus and Cadence, too. I feel responsible for them being taken." A tear wells up in her eye.

I throw my sandwich on my brown bag and pull her close. "It's not your fault. It's not my fault, either. I didn't ask for this to happen, and neither did Tarick, Marcus, or Cadence." Her hair sweeps into her face, and I tuck it behind her ear.

Lisa gives me a half-smile.

"By the way, how is Astid doing at your house?" I ask.

"She's doing fine. Believe it or not, I feel safer with her there. She used her powers on my parents to make them unground me and take a cruise to the Caribbean. At least they will be safe." A little crease forms between Lisa's eyes. "You know, you should really consider having Astid send your mom away for too. Things are just too dangerous around here."

"I can't do that to my mom. It feels wrong manipulating her, and I can't ask Astid to do that, too, but I am happy you're not grounded any longer." I smile and kiss her forehead.

Lisa's not convinced. "Consider it, at least, okay? My parents really needed a vacation anyway. Maybe your mom does, too. I wish we all could just run away."

"I'll think about it," I say half-heartedly. "And if we all just took off, Level 6 would just nab us anyway."

We sit quietly for another minute or two, lost in our own thoughts.

"I wish I could stay longer, but I'm pushing it. I'll see you after school." Lisa kisses me and leaves me alone on the bench.

It feels weird eating at a big table all by myself. I was never the most popular guy in school, but I always had plenty of friends that would sit with me at lunch. Tarick, Cadence, and Marcus always sat with me if they had the same lunch hour. But usually, there would be another two or three buddies at my table.

After Tarick's disappearance, my other friends had stopped calling or texting me. And as I sit here finishing my sandwich all alone, I feel the lingering stares from the other kids. Even guys I used to pal around with look at me as if I have the plague.

Last year, we read *The Scarlet Letter* in American Lit. That's me. Put a big-ass *A* on my chest.

Lisa is the only one that will even blink in my direction. After Cadence and Marcus' disappearance, now even she had mentioned feeling that she was an outcast. It's messed up. I want to shout, *I'm not in a cult!*, but it's no use.

Classes can't end soon enough. Mom didn't call to remind me to go to the therapist. I have a feeling she doesn't want to push me now, especially with Marcus' disappearance.

I'm sure a part of her wanted to ask me questions about Marcus, too, but I dropped a bomb on her instead. I fed her the same line I gave Detective Jennings. I told her that instead of spending the night at Marcus' house, that I stayed at Lisa's. Her parents were out of town, after all.

Amazingly, Mom wasn't too pissed. Maybe it's because I was doing the normal teenager-thing and wanted to spend the night with my first serious girl-friend. Instead of grounding me, she gave me a lecture about safe sex and said she'd bring me some condoms after work. My embarrassment was worth it though. The last thing I need is to have Mom scared of me too.

I feel horrible for Marcus' mom and Cadence's parents. Hopefully, I'll figure something out. Maybe I should go to therapy and see if Dr. Wilson, or what-ever her real name is, will admit the truth and I can bargain with her. I'll help them get whatever it is they want in return for Marcus and Cadence's safety.

I'm practically running out of the school building, and I nearly run over some poor freshman moving too slow out the front doors. I find Lisa's car and wait for her. Again, it's like I might as well not even exist. I see guys I've known since grade school walk past me. Once in a while, someone will glance my way, but they hurry away.

Finally, Lisa's walking down the main steps to the parking lot.

"Hey!" I reach out to her and she walks into my arms. "You took forever."

Lisa gives me a nudge with her elbow. "My last

class is clear on the other side of the building." She unlocks the doors and I get in her Mustang.

"I guess we should go to your house right away," I say. Normally, I'd have some shady intentions saying something like that to a girl. "Plus, I could use your help on an essay for English Lit."

Lisa starts the engine and throws me a smile, but then it quickly evaporates. "I hope Astid is okay. I didn't like leaving her alone."

"I'm sure she's fine," I say.

We weave through traffic and finally get to the main road. With the warm wind coming in from the open windows, I close my eyes to enjoy these next few minutes in peace. But my imagination won't stop running wild. I don't want to imagine what's happening to Marcus and Cadence right now, but the guilt won't leave me alone.

After the ten-minute drive, we arrive at Lisa's house. Right away, an eerie feeling comes over me. The front door sways open, and Astid isn't there waiting for us.

"Let me go in and check. You stay in the car," I say.

Lisa nods. "Mav, be careful." She grabs my left hand and squeezes it.

I jump out of the car and casually walk towards the front porch. The door squeaks when I push it a little further open. "Astid?" I call out. *Astid, damnit, where are you?*

No reply comes, and I slowly slip into the house,

checking behind each door. I'm expecting other BEKs to jump out at me, but there's no buzzing sound in my head, so they must not be around. Maybe those spooks from Level 6 are here and they took Astid. All they wanted was Astid and the other BEKs, and we practically handed her over on a silver platter.

After moving slowly through each room, I find nothing out of place. I'm relieved, yet even more terrified. Where is Astid? Maybe she went to my tree house. I pray there's a simple and harmless explanation for all of this, but I know better than to be so optimistic. I take one final glance at everything before bolting out of Lisa's house and heading back to her car.

"Astid is gone, and there's no sign of her anywhere," I tell Lisa. "You need to take me home now. Something doesn't feel right."

"You think she might have gone back to your house?" Lisa asks. "Maybe she went to your old tree house. That would be okay, right? Isn't your mom still at work?"

A cold ice pick of terror runs straight through my chest. I pull my phone from my pocket and speed dial Mom's cell. I get back into Lisa's car as the phone rings before going to her voice mail. I try her work number. Lisa pulls out of the drive way and gets back on the main road. No answer at work either.

"I can't get a hold of her," I say.

"I'm sure she's fine. She'll call you back any

minute." Lisa speeds up but is careful to not go more than five miles an hour over the speed limit. "I'm worried about Astid, though. Hopefully she's waiting for us at your tree house."

When we enter my development, my stomach lurches at the sight of Mom's car in the driveway. She's already home from work, and it's too early for her. "I hope she's feeling okay. She never leaves work early unless she's sick."

My words sound even and calm, but I'm already sweating. My brain fills with the frantic buzzing of killer bees. Before Lisa can kill the engine, I rush out of the car and dash up the driveway. I throw open the door. In the living room, Astid's on one knee. She's next to Mom who lays still on the floor.

Maverick, I'm so sorry. Tears stream from her big black eyes.

"What did you do to her?" I run into the room and bend down to wake her up. "Mom?" I shake her, but she doesn't respond at all. Her body is limp. "Wake up, Mom!" Her eyes are closed, but her mouth is drawn slightly open.

I put my ear to her chest to listen for a heartbeat, but I hear nothing but my own heavy breathing. When I touch her pale face, her skin is ice cold.

"Astid?" Lisa's in the doorway, her hand cups her mouth to stifle a scream.

Astid straightens up and backs up against the wall. *I was too late, I'm so sorry.*

"What are you saying? She's not dead. She's sleeping," I shake her harder now. "Mom! Mom! Wake up, damnit!"

"Oh my God!" Lisa rushes to my side. "Maverick, I'll call an ambulance."

"You did this!" I scream at Astid.

She shakes her head. *No Maverick, I didn't. I'm so sorry. I couldn't save her. She was already gone when I got here.*

"NO! NO! NO!" I taste murder on my tongue, and I want to kill every single black-eyed freak in the world. "GET OUT OF MY HOUSE!"

I pull Mom's listless body up into my arms. "Mom! Mom! Wake up now!" A trickle of blood flows from her mouth. I pull open her eyelids, and jump at the sight of them. My body shakes uncontrollably as I stare into her blood-filled eyes.

Lisa screams and looks away, and she gasps for air in between sobs.

Mom's not sleeping. She is dead.

31

ASTID

HE TREE HOUSE seems cold and lonely. The clouds look like tiny starbursts exploding as the sun descends on the western horizon. The agony overflowing in Maverick's mind rips me apart, and the pain courses from his body to mine. Instead of essential energy flowing, it's pure emotional poison.

It's so strong, it reaches me here, even when I've never been able to feel someone from this far away before. He's still home, crying and exploding with rage.

When Mother died, I recall the brief moment of sadness, but we expected her death. The heavy, horrible feelings streaming through Maverick now are a hundred times worse. His bond with his mother was far greater than the one I had with my own mother.

Maverick might believe my brother and the others did it, but I know better. Kren would never have allowed the body to remain, but perhaps he is angrier than I'd imagined. Maybe he left evidence of his cruelty in order to send me a message.

That's unlikely, however. I'm certain it wasn't Kren who took Maverick's mother's life. There's only one other possible cause, and it's too terrifying to contemplate.

MAVERICK

O N MY DRIVEWAY, the paramedics cover Mom with the white sheet, and the finality of it sets in. She's gone and she's not coming back. She's dead because of me...no, because of *them*. Those demon-eyed monsters took her away from me. She didn't deserve any of this. All she wanted was to protect me, and now this is what happens?

It's not fair.

Lisa touches my shoulder. "Mav, let's go inside."

"Do you have any family in town you can stay with?" Detective Jennings asks. "Someone I can call for you?"

Lisa shakes her head. "His dad lives in Indiana," she tells him. "We need to call him."

Tears roll from her eyes, but I'm in no shape to console her.

"Can you stay with a friend? An adult that will stay with you or allow you to stay with them?"

Detective Jennings' voice sounds sincere, less severe than the previous times he's dealt with me.

I'm amazed he's not cuffing me and throwing me in the slammer. I know I would if I were him. Three friends missing and now this…any sane person would peg me as guilty. They must think I'm a serial murderer by now.

Luckily, school officials were able to confirm that me and Lisa were at school all day. Otherwise, I know I'd be in jail.

Through my despair, I decide that I have no choice but to turn to the one person who'll understand my situation better than anyone else will. "Ronald Tunstall," I say. "He's a friend of the family, and he's in town. I'm sure he'll stay with me."

"Let's give him a call then and inform your father of the circumstances," Detective Jennings says.

Circumstances? Is my mother's death just a circumstance? Heat begins to build under my skin.

I grit my teeth, holding back the stream of profanities that threaten to erupt from my shaking lips. "I'll tell my father what's happened here, and then I'll call Ronald for help."

Jennings nods and leads Lisa away from me so he can talk with her in private. She pulls out her phone with trembling hands. The detective looks sympathetic.

I get my own phone out and find Dad's number, but I just can't do it. He'll freak out and rush down here right away. Getting Dad involved might get him killed too. Instead, I find Ronald's card on my dresser and call him.

Ronald answers, and all I say is, "They killed my mother."

He asks me a few pertinent questions about my parents so that he can get his story to the cops straight. Then he says sorry about a dozen times before telling me to wait for him.

The next hour is a blur. Amazingly, Detective Jennings doesn't arrest me. Instead, he hangs around with some other cops in the living room.

Ronald arrives an hour or so later, and I continue to pace in my room. The detective refused to leave until he arrived, and Lisa took it upon herself to wait with Jennings, right near where my mother lay dead not two hours before.

"Where is he?" Ronald asks as he enters, his voice carrying down the hall.

I hear heavy footsteps coming towards me, and Ronald stops just inside my doorway. My fists ache from being balled for so long, and I release them at my side.

"Was it…?" he asks, but doesn't finish the question.

I nod, and Ronald enters my bedroom. He takes quick steps towards me and embraces me tightly with his thick arms.

Despite my best to keep it together, I lose it all over again.

THE SUN BREAKS through the window and hits my eyelids. I didn't think it was possible to fall asleep, but I must have cried my way into exhaustion. Last night felt like such a nightmare, as if it didn't really happen.

Jennings and the police hung around for a long time, talking with Ronald for a bit until they left. He did leave to get some sandwiches for us, but I didn't take one bite. The last thing I remember was crawling into bed.

It's now morning, and nothing but dread greets me when I wake up.

Ronald slumps over in the beanbag chair, with a revolver sitting on his lap. Lisa pushes up against my back, and I'm thankful she stayed with me through the night.

I sit up, and Lisa rouses awake.

"Mav?" she says, her voice cracking.

"Yeah?" I ask, sitting up.

"We need to call your dad." She rises onto her elbows. "He'll know what to do about your…"

"No!" Ronald shakes himself fully awake, and he clutches his gun. "If your father comes to town, he'll be in danger, too."

I wholeheartedly agree. "That's exactly why I didn't call him."

"So, what are you planning on doing?" Lisa asks me.

"We need to find the BEKs and end this." I walk out the door and into my mom's room to her closet. "I'm tired of being such a coward."

"Find the BEKs?" Lisa asks from the doorway.

"Kid, you're angry at the moment, and I totally understand that," Ronald says. "Believe me, I've been there. I get it."

"Do you?" I find the key to the safe, hidden right under her jewelry boxes in the armoire. "You should know exactly how I feel, Ronald. They took your wife and son, just like they did with my friends and my mom." I point at him. "You should be just as angry as I am, and believe me, when you hear the truth, you'll be even angrier."

"What are you talking about?" he asks.

I unlock the gun safe and find my father's pistol, the one he left to protect the family. The one he taught me and Mom how to use.

The one I plan to use to kill those black-eyed kids.

33

MAVERICK

"WHOA KID, I'M not sure this is the best way to handle things. Why don't you put that away?" Ronald follows me around Mom's room while I pace back and forth. "And explain to me just what is going on here. Those BEKs obviously returned to your house, but why?"

Ronald scratches his head and runs his hand over the few remaining hairs to pat them down. He looks at me as if he suspects that I know something he doesn't know, and it's pissing him off.

"We know things, Ronald, and now we're a liability." I grab the two additional magazines and close the gun safe back up.

"Maybe we should go back to my house first," Lisa says. "I'm not so sure it's entirely safe to stay here much longer."

Last night, Lisa wanted us to go to her house too, but I just couldn't leave. It was as if I kept expecting

Mom to still be in her room, laying in bed watching TV.

I turn to her. "Ronald needs to know, too. He's just as involved as we are, and he's probably lucky he's still alive. Especially since my therapist knows exactly who he is."

"What are you talking about? What therapist?" Ronald asks. "Tell me everything."

With the gun and ammo in my pocket, I rush past him and head for the living room. Ronald is right on my heels, and I can hear him breathing heavily. I step around the spot on the floor where Mom's body had been, and I sit on the couch.

"Let's start with the black-eyed kids," I say in a low voice. "They aren't from another planet or another dimension. They aren't some unknown species that have lived here for eternity like vampires. Those freaks were created by *us*. Our own government created them."

"How do you know this?" Ronald asks.

"Because one of them told me," I reply. "Astid. She's the BEK that actually released me from the barn the night Tarick was killed. She told me all about Level 6. It's some government facility that houses strange and bizarre experiments, and they used human subjects. They messed with their genetics, and the black-eyed kids are a direct result."

Ronald plops down next to me. "You're kidding me, right?" He looks up at me, his eyes searching for the truth. "And you mean to tell me that one of the black-eyed kids, a female named Astid, told you all this?"

Lisa remains standing near the front door, as if she's going to run away any second. "We're telling you the truth."

"I'm not lying," I assure him. "One of the agents pretended to be my new therapist, and she's basically using us as bait to get to the BEKs who escaped from their secret facility. Only she ended up kidnapping our friends, Cadence and Marcus, in the process."

I pause to let that sink into Ronald's head for a little while. He stares up at the ceiling, connecting the dots from his own investigation. Either that, or he's about to have a nervous breakdown.

"Level 6 agents could be watching us right now," I say. "Who knows what they did with Cadence and Marcus. And now, the BEKs killed my mom."

Ronald wipes the sweat from his big forehead. "Look, I believe you, but some stuff just doesn't add up here. BEKs never stay in the area for long. They hightail it shortly after several disappearances hit the radar. And what you're telling me about the government involvement...that makes sense. But what about the Astid BEK. She just willingly spilled the beans about everything?"

My eyes drop back down to the spot where I found Mom. I don't care if it all adds up or not. We all know who killed her, and that's all that matters to me.

"Astid is one of them, but she's the one who let me go that night in the barn."

Ronald nods his head. "Okay, so that explains how you escaped. But why would she do that? Why would she be telling you everything and helping you?"

"Because she's different," Lisa replies. "She refuses to go along with the other black-eyed kids."

"We need to get this information to a safe source." Ronald pulls out his phone. "What else do you know about Level 6?"

That's the exact moment the eerie feeling creeps back in, and the buzzing in my head begins. Lisa and Ronald both put their hands to their ears.

Ronald turns around to face the doorway and pulls his gun.

Kren and his buddies are back.

34

ASTID

NO! THEY'RE NEAR. I can feel their energy invading Maverick's mind. Kren stands at the edge of the forest behind Maverick's house. Avion and Garn linger nearby, and they're watching Maverick.

Kren!

It's no use. He knows I'm close, and he blocks my thoughts from entering his mind. Instead, I turn my attention back to Maverick. I concentrate for only a moment before I sense his fury. Somehow, he's not affected by the mind invasion like Lisa and the other man named Ronald are.

Maverick's anger builds until it takes over his senses. He's filled with only one thought...revenge.

He races from the house, aiming a weapon at Kren and the others, but they fan out too quickly. Maverick knows they are too fast for him, but his hatred pushes him forward. Amazingly, my mind connection with him breaks. It's as if Maverick also blocks me from his thoughts.

How can that be?

No human can do that.

I jump from the tree house and dart in their direction, but by the time I reach his house, Kren already has Maverick in his grasp. A gun lays several feet away in the grass. Ronald steps out into the yard holding his own weapon, and Lisa trails behind him.

I confront Kren directly. "No!"

Garn and Avion appear on either side of me. They grab my arms, and I lack the strength to escape. Kren tightens his grip on Maverick's throat. I struggle for a moment, but it's no use. Maverick and his friends will die, and it will be my fault.

"Let the boy go." Ronald's stern voice cracks. He thrusts his gun forward, but he looks to be in pain. His eyes narrow, and his breathing becomes shallow. "I *will* shoot you."

Lisa and Ronald are in agony as our natural energy already penetrates their brains. Maverick's mouth is drawn open, gasping for breath. Kren's fingers nearly cut off his air.

I hear Kren's thoughts shoot through me. *You chose these weaklings over us?*

There is only one way to save Maverick. *Kren, you have me, now let them go. I'll go back with you and die with honor.*

Kren shakes his head. *This wasn't about you dying.*

All I wanted was for you to live. You have betrayed our family. You have betrayed me.

The last of what little strength I have fades away, and I can't even hold my head up. *I know. But I'm here now. Please let them go. Please, I'm begging you.*

Maverick lets out a gasp when Kren's pale fingers tighten. *Why do you care about them so much? You see their cruelty and emotions and how they are ruled by them. This man with the gun would kill me in a split second. He's no different from the ones who kept us imprisoned for so long.*

My vision blurs, and I feel like I might pass out. *They are different. Our mother was human, remember? I want you to spare them because they showed me kindness. Despite the death of his best friend, Maverick allowed me to stay with them, learn from them. They are not all evil. Let him go.*

Maverick tries to tear himself away and struggles under Kren's strength. "You killed my mom, you bastard!"

Kren's eyes widen. *We didn't kill his mother.*

My mind reaches out to my brother, and he allows my energy to pass through his defenses. Instantly, I know that he is being truthful. *His mother was taken last night. Her life force was drained, but her physical body remained. I thought you were to blame.*

It was not us. Kren's grip loosens just enough for Maverick to take a deeper breath in and out. *You know this is true.*

35

MAVERICK

MY THROAT BURNS as the air struggles to move in and out of my lungs. The pain is a welcome feeling, a distraction to the swarm buzzing in my head. My legs drag against the dirt as this black-eyed demon pulls me deeper into the woods.

Ronald, with his gun drawn and pointed straight in our direction, follows us. Lisa remains at his side, and I want to yell at her to go back into the house, but no words can escape my lips.

The pure strength of this kid is terrifying. Kren looks ten years younger than me, yet he's yanking my body around like a rag doll.

Kren, please stop this! Astid chimes into our heads once again, pleading with her brother. The sound of her thoughts lessens the noise echoing between my ears.

Astid struggles against the other two boys, but she looks too weak to fight back.

"Stop!" Ronald roars, and Kren backs up against a tree to face him.

Astid's arms are gripped tightly by two other black-eyed kids who are just as terrifying as Kren. The taller, pale-faced freak appears to be closer to our age. His face turns toward me, and he sneers with his lips rising at the corners.

The boy on the other side of Astid is shorter and looks younger, but his black eyes remain focused on Ronald's gun.

Choose! Kren shouts into our heads. He swivels towards Astid.

I have chosen, Astid replies. *Why can't you accept that?*

Kren's grip on the back of my neck tightens and he thrusts me up into the air. My feet leave the ground, and I feel so helpless against Astid's brother.

I'm not sure if Kren projects his thoughts into all of our heads, or if I'm somehow intercepting them.

You cower from your destiny. You want to save your friend? Then choose who will die in his place. Kren looks at Ronald and Lisa. *The girl or the old man?*

Astid shakes her head. *No!*

I try again to free myself from Kren, but the more I resist, the tighter his grip becomes. I feel like I'm going to black out.

Kren bangs his fist against the tree trunk, sending cones and needles falling to the ground.

Ronald flinches and retreats. "Let him go!" He steps forward again, his gun rattling in both hands.

Kren signals to the tall, skinny black-eyed monster next to Astid. In an instant, the teenager streaks across the damp grass and appears at Ronald's side. He tears the pistol from Ronald's grasp and throws the gun to the ground several feet away.

Ronald falls to his knees in front of the BEK, and his eyes become hollow. It's like I'm watching Tarick on the floor of his house all over again. Astid tries to pull away from the shorter kid, but she can't break free.

My voice erupts. "NO!"

Lisa screams, and the tall one turns his attention toward her. She shuts her mouth as if a ghostly hand grasps her lips and seals them together. She struggles against an invisible force clutching her throat.

Kren's thoughts penetrate my brain. *Avion, cease!*

Avion circles behind Ronald and Lisa. They both collapse onto the ground. Lisa crawls toward Ronald, grabbing onto his arm.

Astid, my patience is thinning. The choice is yours. You will choose one of them, or they will all die. Kren pulls me toward him and looks me straight in the face. Our eyes meet, and his black orifices bore into me. A darkness encompasses my entire view, as if I've suddenly gone blind. The swarm in my head grows so loud, my eardrums are about to explode.

Somehow, I can still hear Astid's thoughts. *Not Maverick, please, I beg you.*

I can feel Kren's breath on my forehead.

Choose now, or he dies.

My head pounds, and my eyes feel like they might pop out of their sockets. The night begins to fade around me, revealing blurry greens and browns.

While remaining on his knees, Ronald's blurry image creeps towards Kren with both hands still cupping his ears. "Take me."

I'm not sure, but I think I black out for a few seconds. A sharp pain shoots through my body and settles back up into my brain. The agony takes my breath away, but I'm relieved that I'm still conscious.

Kren opens his mouth. "Do it, Sister!"

His voice sounds rough, as if broken glass lines his throat and scratches his words.

Tears flow from Astid's black eyes. She drags her feet toward Ronald and bends down to him, her chest heaving in tiny intervals. Kren's hold on my throat loosens just enough for me to take several deep breaths.

Lisa scoots away from Ronald as Astid approaches. Her sobs start small, but she's sobbing when she figures out what's happening.

Ronald turns toward me, his drooping eyes plead with me. "Kid, get the information to the right people in my group."

I can only blink my eyes rapidly to let him know I understand.

"On my computer…email…" His voice fades. His hands ball up into tight fists as he looks into Astid's deep, black eyes. "It's okay…"

Astid's thoughts come through. *I'm sorry, Ronald.*

The humming in my mind ceases. The sounds of the forest let me know that I'm not permanently deaf. I can hear everything. A soft breeze makes the tree branches rattle. The chirping of crickets almost becomes deafening. Something is different. My vision sharpens, as if I can see in the dark.

"I know," Ronald says out loud. But his mouth doesn't move. Did he think those words? *I don't blame you, Astid.*

Lisa's horrified thoughts come to me. *Oh God, Oh God, Oh God...*

She's not moving her lips either. Lisa remains on the ground, backed up against the tree with her back pushed into the bark. What is going on? Kren must have done something to my brain.

Now I can hear...*everyone's* thoughts?

Astid reaches out and takes Ronald's face in between her hands. Her eyes meet his. When her mouth opens, Ronald does likewise. The fear melts away from his face. His expression matches Astid's exactly, and they both wear the look of determination on their identical faces.

I feel Astid's black energy enter his mind, trapping him in the abyss of her power. He's helpless to escape. It's as if his whole being has been captured by the surging power coming from her. Two beams of light shoot out of both of his eyes and go directly into Astid's dark pools. Ronald's life force is being sucked away.

Blood flows from his ears and then his nose. The

vessels in his eyes pop, and the whites of his eyes turn red. The color in his flesh fades away as the two rays of light intensify, illuminating the entire forest.

I can't bear to watch anymore. Somehow, I can feel Ronald's storm of emotions. Regret replaces his fear. And his final thoughts turn to his wife and son. A big part of him is relieved that he will finally be reunited with them.

A fierce white light surrounds Astid's body. Despite my eyes being shut as tight as I can make them, the light penetrates them and I'm forced to turn my head away. Lisa lets out a muffled scream as the light grows in intensity.

A moment later, Ronald is gone.

The darkness returns.

When I open my eyes, I'm expecting to see Ronald's body on the ground. Instead, a small pile of ashes remain where he had been kneeling. Astid stands over it, and her shoulders are heaving.

Kren's hand remains around my neck, but his fingers have loosened enough for me to maybe try to wiggle free. I'm too scared to try, though.

Astid turns around, and it's clear that she's not crying. Her fists clench, and her black eyes narrow. A tide of hot-red energy surrounds her petite body.

I don't need a psychic link to know what Astid wants.

Kren and his goons are *so* screwed.

ASTID

I T HAS BEEN so long since energy such as this has flowed through my body. The intensity touches every inch of me. The power forms inside, growing more each second, and then the euphoria sets in.

This feeling is different, though. It's stronger than I've ever felt before. Maybe it's because I have not consumed life in such a long time. I feel invincible.

I stare at Ronald's ashes on the ground. Surging power and anger hardens my resolve-anger at being forced to take another innocent life, even though that life has now provided for me. I feel a tear trickle from my eye. Ronald has sacrificed everything for us, and his bravery inspires me.

Welcome back. Kren's voice penetrates my thoughts, and my fury deepens.

I turn to face him, and the grin on his face washes away. There is no hiding my thoughts, and I feel his fear. He has crossed the line by forcing me to feed, and the boiling rage inside me erupts.

Maverick breaks free and crawls away from Kren, and my brother launches himself deeper into the woods. He's fast, but I'm faster. I reach out and grab his shoulder.

Kren's feet kick out beneath him as I lift him into the air. He swats at my arm, but his strength is no match for mine. Rapid footsteps approach from behind, and as I turn, Avion crashes into me. My grip on Kren loosens. I tumble forward and slam into the ground. Kren rolls away and springs back onto his feet quickly.

Avion jumps on top of me and tries to pin me to the ground, but he can't hold me for long. I push him off after a short struggle. I move to grab his wrists and straddle his squirming body.

The craving overcomes me. I almost let Avion go, but he will fight until one of us dies. He tries to get free, but it's no use. Somehow, my strength increases, and I can feel his bones in my hands on the verge of shattering.

Avion's eyes meet mine, and he stops struggling. My power has taken total control over him. His mind goes blank, and numbness begins to take over his body.

Garn tries to pull at me from behind, but he's too late. There's no prying me from the energy flow.

ASTID, STOP! Kren screams. His thoughts pour into my head. *This is madness. Stop this right now. Let him go. He's one of us. You can't do this. You are betraying your own!*

Kren touches my shoulder, but the burst of energy pushes him away. He reaches out to Avion, but his fingers spark, and Kren cries out. The link is complete. No one can separate us now.

More of my brother's words ring into my head, but the energy bursts muffle them. After another few seconds, I can only hear a vibrating hum that grows louder and louder. My body feels like it's floating in the air, so light and free, ready to escape the earthly confinement in which we've been trapped for far too long.

As if I've reached the apex of ecstasy, I feel the rushing of the breeze grow, and it thrashes against my skin as I fall back toward the ground. I'm falling very, very fast. It's as if my wings have been clipped and I can no longer ride the waves of the wind.

37

MAVERICK

M Y LUNGS ARE on fire, and I still struggle to take in air. As I go in the direction of where black-eyed kids ran, my courage diminishes with every step. Maybe following them into the forest is a bad idea. The moment I see Astid on top of the other BEK, I stop in my tracks.

I back away from the scene, slamming into the trunk of a tall tree. Its bark scratches against my skin. I cover my eyes, but only for a second. I can't look away either. The buzzing in my head intensifies until I'm sure my brain is about to explode.

The furious look on Astid's face transforms to one of bliss. Kren tries to break them up a couple times, but he yelps as if a bolt of electricity shoots up his arm every time he touches either one of them. Astid's face reddens, and that tall black-eyed kid withers away while in her grasp.

He disintegrates to a pile of ashes, and Astid falls

away from them and onto her back. Her brother and the other one stand motionless for a moment. Oh crap, are they going to kill her now? And then kill me?

Kren's already pale face somehow turns a lighter shade of white. He's frightened of his sister! The pair of black-eyed kids exchange panicked looks and dart away.

In my head, the bees begin to quiet slowly, giving way to a moment of complete silence. Astid stares at the pile of ashes next to her.

I turn to look for Lisa, but she's nowhere in sight. "Lisa?" I cup my hands over my face, and yell louder, "LISA!"

My head spins in every direction, searching her out. I wonder if she ran home during all of the fighting. I wouldn't blame her; I remember her thoughts. Her thoughts were so clear to me a moment ago, the terror seizing her whole being after seeing what happened to Ronald. I can only hope that Lisa is safe at my house.

Astid looks exhausted, yet determined.

"Astid?" I scoot a little closer but keep my distance. "Are you all right?" It's a stupid question, but I don't know what else to say.

I'm kind of afraid of her. The gentle and compassionate Astid I knew evaporates in front of my eyes. I had no idea she was capable of such rage. And I could actually feel her anger toward her brother. For a brief moment, I swore we were mentally connected.

I want Astid to destroy Kren. Revenge for killing Tarick and Ronald was the only thing on my mind, and somehow, she and I shared our hatred for her brother. But I didn't expect her to be so…savage.

Maverick. She looks toward me, and her black eyes have changed. Instead of the pure black abyss of nothingness, it's as if a swirling mass of puffy white and gray clouds have entered into them, mixing with the black. It looks like tiny tornadoes have invaded her eye sockets. I can't look away.

"Do you know what happened to Lisa?" I ask. "Can you sense her neaby? Did she run back toward the house?"

Astid sits up and wipes away some of the dirt from her face but ends up smearing it across her checks. She looks around and holds her head in her hands, squeezing her eyes shut. She moves her palms to her eyes and rubs them.

No, she's not at your house. She opens her eyes and looks at me. The swirls in her eyes slow their spinning, and the black begins to cover the white and gray areas.

"Your eyes are so…" The word escapes me. They look so mesmerizing and scary all at the same time. She looks away from me, blinking them shut.

Where is my brother? she asks. She stands and begins to assess her surroundings.

I dare to step closer to her. "I'm not sure. They ran off in that direction super-fast once they saw what you did to their friend." I point to the ashes that continue to be swept away in the breeze. "Are you okay?"

I'm fine.

Astid's facial expression tells me differently, and her emotions seep from her mind into mine.

She can't sense her brother and the other BEK, and it bothers her. She can't sense anyone. She's searching for Lisa, for Kren, and...for the other BEK named Garn. Her frustration flows into me as if I'm reading her thoughts right out of a book.

"Holy crap!" I blurt out, realizing that I'm reading her mind just the way she reads mine and it freaks me out.

Maverick, I don't know where they are...any of them.

I do! A strange voice echoes in our heads at the same time.

"Who was that?" I press my head with both hands. I'm not liking this telepathy crap. "That wasn't your brother, was it?"

Astid replies with her mouth, "No."

The unknown voice invades our minds again. *If you want to see Lisa alive again, come to the very place where this whole thing started. I can't guarantee she'll be alive for much longer.*

I can't explain how I know, but it dawns on me who is reaching out to us telepathically. It's Cadence.

Cadence just spoke to us.

38

MAVERICK

CADENCE'S VOICE LINGERS in my head when a wave of loud static fills my ears. And then nothing.

"Did you hear that?" I don't have to ask, because I know Astid did too.

They have Lisa. Astid says. *At the barn.* She turns to go in that direction, but I grab onto her arm to stop her.

A sharp electric current shocks me, and I snap my hand back quickly.

"Wow, did you feel that?" I ask.

Astid rubs the area I grabbed. *Yes, I did.*

"That was Cadence talking to us," I say. "But, how?"

I'm not entirely sure. Yet.

She's keeping something from me, but I'm in no position to interrogate her. I start towards my house, and Astid follows right behind me. I look around and spot the very thing I need. Ronald's gun. I reach down and grab it before rushing to catch up with Astid.

You should stay here, and I'll go to the barn. It's too dangerous. You need to get inside your house and wait for me.

"If those Level 6 spooks have my friends, I need to help you save them." I turn the gun over and wipe it on my shirt. I remember the safety, and click it to the off position.

Didn't you hear Cadence? She wasn't warning you, she was threatening us. Astid turns around and starts walking away. *She is no longer the Cadence you know. They have turned her.*

I don't want to believe her, but I know that the voice was threatening, and it sounded so…weird. But it was distinctively Cadence. I'm still confused about how she was able to talk to us telepathically, but at this point, I'm confused about everything. I try my best to keep up with Astid.

Just go home and wait. I will take care of everything, she says telepathically.

"Astid, I have nothing to go home to. All that I care about is in that direction." I point towards the woods. "We're wasting time here, so let's go."

She doesn't protest, and we jog toward the place I was hoping to never see again.

THE MIDDAY SUN beats down on us, and the light breeze that flowed moments ago stops. The closer we get to the barn, the more my nerves kick in, and I begin to shake.

The gun feels heavy in my hand, and I make sure that the barrel points toward the ground. I don't know how many bullets are in the magazine, but I do feel more powerful with it.

Once we pass over the road, adrenaline starts pumping through my veins. A mass of voices begin to pound into my head, and they all mix together that I can't make out one coherent thought among them. I don't understand what is happening to me, but I don't have time to freak out about it.

"Astid," I whisper. "There's a bunch of people up ahead."

I slow down and try to be quiet as I step on top of the pine needles under foot.

It's a trap, and they know we are near, Astid says. *Two agents are positioned around the barn, both with dart guns. They want me.*

My concentration centers on one of the voices among the many. "My therapist is there. I mean, the female agent, Dr. Wilson...she's waiting for us in the center."

Maverick, you are reading them too. Astid turns her black eyes towards me. *How?*

"I have no idea," I reply. "I can read you, too, but it's harder with them since they are further away." At that moment, I get a clear thought from Lisa.

I'm going to die tonight...I'm going to die, and my parents will never know what happened to me. Lisa's terror turns into sadness. She's accepted that she will not make it through the night, and agony grips me.

The barn is just on the other side of the ridge. Astid and I remain hidden in the thick of the forest.

My knees feel wobbly. "Can you stop the agents while I get Dr. Wilson's attention?" I ask.

Astid nods. *We need to be fast.*

Before she takes off, I grab her arm again, and my hand feels as if I've shoved it into an electrical socket. I shake the feeling back into my fingers.

"Astid?"

She looks at me.

"I'm sorry about what you had to do back there. I know you never wanted to do that ever again. I'm so sorry. I just wanted you to know that."

I know. It's not your fault, and I'm sorry you and your friends got involved with all of this. You are one of the good ones, Maverick. We will get through this, I promise you.

I want to give her one last hug, but I'm pretty sure my arms would get fried.

I point towards the barn. "Wait for me on the hill. As soon as I distract the agents, you go in and...do your Wonder Woman thing."

Astid's a blur when she rushes towards the ridge before diving onto the ground.

I take several deep breaths before I leave the

safety of the woods. I run straight to the front of the barn and come face-to-face with something more terrifying than Kren himself.

39

ASTID

MY BODY FEELS like it's on fire. The scorching power courses through my veins. Kren and Garn are nowhere in the vicinity, and I know it's only a matter of time before I need to go after them, but right now, I need to help Maverick save Lisa. She's so frightened, and her fear has sunk to sorrow.

I stay laying on my stomach as I peer over the ridge. One agent with dark skin guards Lisa. I can't see the other one, but I can sense him standing around the other corner of the barn with a pistol in his hands. Lisa's crying, but the agent remains unmoved.

Far to my left, Maverick runs from the forest towards the front of the barn. The two men guarding Lisa swivel towards Maverick with their guns. I leap to my feet and rush towards Lisa. I pounce on the guard, snatching his gun and throwing it away.

He tries to punch me, but I capture his fist in my hand. He yelps in pain. I subdue him with my mind's power. I don't have time to consume him. Instead, I strike a quick blow to his head. His neck cracks before he crumples to the ground.

Lisa gasps and presses up against the barn. I turn to see what she's looking at and catch movement coming towards us.

Cadence turns the corner.

Her black eyes narrow at me. I allow myself to feel pity for her. Cadence is no longer human.

Another agent leaps out from behind her and fires his gun before I'm able to move. Just as the dart jabs my arm, a crack of thunder from behind fills the sky. I fall to my knees, and the agent who had shot me clutches his chest before he staggers backwards.

MAVERICK

PANIC SEIZES ME as Astid goes down, and my hands won't stop shaking. I aim my gun at Dr. Wilson.

"Don't even think about it, Maverick," Dr. Wilson says. My part-time psychiatrist grabs Lisa and places the pistol against her temple.

I lower my gun.

"Good boy." Dr. Wilson turns toward Cadence, and that's when Marcus appears next to her.

They look like my friends, but there's something...off. "Marcus? Cadence?" I squint my eyes to get a better look at them. "What's going on?"

Cadence and Marcus come toward me, and that's when I see their faces more clearly. My knees buckle. Their black eyes stare back at me, and they look angry.

"Mav, dude, you shouldn't have come here."

Marcus cocks his head to the side. "You should have just stayed out of the way."

Marcus' voice sounds weird. I recognize it, but it's all wrong. His words are deliberate and full of tension.

"You killed my mom, didn't you?" As soon as the words escape my lips, I already know the answer. I see the whole thing in his mind. It's like a horrible movie I can't stop myself from watching. I see my mom staring up at Cadence while Marcus looks on.

"She was delicious," Cadence says with a smile.

My eyes sting from tears pouring from them. "What happened to you? I can't believe…Cadence, you killed her?"

My friends are better off dead. I don't know what sick experiment Level 6 did on them, but Cadence and Marcus no longer exist.

"You're wrong, Maverick," Cadence says. "This is ten times better, and we will live forever."

"What are you talking about?" I ask.

"They gave us eternal life." Cadence nods toward Dr. Wilson. "We're powerful in every way. Even Marcus is smarter."

I'm reluctant to approach them, but I do anyway. "You're wrong, Cadence. It's a curse. You will have to kill innocent people to stay alive." I turn to Marcus. "How could you kill my mom?"

Marcus' black eyes fall towards the ground, and for a split second, I see a glimpse of my old friend.

"Man, it wasn't…I didn't want to." Marcus struggles, and Cadence hits him in the gut.

Stop moping you imbecile, she tells him mentally. *This is the best possible high you can get.*

Marcus grunts and looks back at me, his sad black eyes give me no answers. Neither of them know I can read their thoughts, so I'm hoping I can use that to my advantage and come out of this alive.

Dr. Wilson keeps the gun pressed to Lisa's head. "We don't need him. Kill him."

"This is wrong," I say, waving my hands up and backing away. I swivel towards Dr. Wilson. "Let Lisa go! She has nothing to do with this."

Cadence inches toward me, her wicked smile creeps up the side of her face. "Orders are orders."

I can hear Marcus' reluctant thoughts. *Cadence, maybe this is wrong. He's our friend.*

Good to see my buddy Marcus is still alive in there behind his black eyes, but Cadence looks like she's ready to devour me whole.

Cadence telepathically tells him, *He left us to this fate, as he left Tarick to die.* She continues coming toward me, and her already black eyes darken.

Her evil whirlpools lock on mine, but there's no buzzing in my head. Not like when Kren had his evil grip on me. It's more like a harmless, faraway ring of a telephone, though I can feel Cadence trying to invade my brain.

She shakes her head and wonders why I'm not on my knees.

Playing along, I drop to the ground without taking my eyes away from her, and her mind eases a little. I pretend to be writhing in agony, but at the moment, I only feel a little fuzzy. Kren's mental grip was a billion times stronger. Blood isn't rushing to my head, but the closer she gets, the weaker I feel.

I try to send Marcus and Cadence one last mental message. *We're best friends. You can't do this to us. These government agents are controlling your minds.*

Cadence stands over me and pulls me up by my collar. She's strong, but not nearly as strong as Astid. I begin to panic as no immediate plan comes to mind when her mental grasp finally latches onto me.

Her eyes swirl with her dark energy. My limbs relax and I know that I'm about to die. Her power has entered my whole being, and I can feel my life begin to slip from my body. Just when I'm about to black out, the power surge comes to an abrupt halt. Cadence's grip loosens, and she collapses on top of me.

The darkness in my mind begins to clear, and I push Cadence's limp body off me. A knife protrudes from her back. Marcus stands over her, trembling. He looks down at me.

"She was going to kill you, man."

Whatever control these government goons had on Cadence, they failed with my man Marcus.

"Guess that ruins my chances of scoring a date with her," Marcus adds. He's still shaken up, but he musters a weak smile.

Dr. Wilson points her gun at Marcus while keeping Lisa in a choke hold with other other arm.

Marcus backs up, and I don't need telepathy to feel the fear growing inside of him. Dr. Wilson pulls a small device from her pocket and pushes a button. Marcus convulses in pain and crumples to the ground. His body squirms until he's still.

"We'll have to work on him a little more," Dr. Wilson says.

I don't care if she's holding a gun. I take several big steps towards her. "You killed him!"

"Your friend made a poor test subject anyway. Too much tetrahydrocannabinol in his system when we did the conversion. Messed with his hippocampus, I assume. Yet another reason to say no to drugs." Dr. Wilson points her gun at me. "Nothing personal, Mr. Ashe. But our national security is at risk."

I shut my eyes, expecting to be struck by the inevitable. Lisa unleashes a scream so loud, I'm wondering if Dr. Wilson has a silencer on her pistol.

The loud boom rips through the air, and I brace myself for the bullet that will end my life. I can hear quick footsteps approaching, and I open my eyes to see Lisa turning away from me.

I peer over her shoulder. Dr. Wilson is on the ground, completely still. Detective Jennings comes up from behind her, still holding his revolver.

41

MAVERICK

DETECTIVE JENNINGS LOOKS like he's about to be sick, and the thoughts roaming through his head consist of him hoping Level 6 doesn't come after him now. I concentrate harder and try to fully read his thoughts.

The cop had witnessed the entire thing. When he looks up at me, his feelings turn to regret. He regrets thinking I was crazy when I told him that the black-eyed kids had killed Tarick.

The BEKs are actually real.

Lisa throws her arms around Jennings. She's sobbing loudly, and it pains me a little that she didn't come to me first. But all of this is my fault. I should never have gotten any of my friends involved.

Marcus stirs near me and clutches his head. "What a bitch, man."

I'm too relieved to find him still alive to be fearful

of his weird black eyes. Even his voice sounds normal. Marcus is still Marcus, somehow.

Detective Jennings pushes Lisa aside and draws his firearm, pointing the gun at Marcus.

"Whoa!" I hold up my hands and put myself between Jennings and my friend. "He's not one of the bad ones, I swear it. He saved my life just now."

"He's one of them." Detective Jennings points toward Astid laying on the ground. "His eyes are all black like hers." His face softens. "And I'm so sorry, Maverick. I'm sorry I didn't believe you. But, would you have believed all of this?"

I shake my head. "Then believe me now, Detective. This is Marcus, one of my friends who went missing, remember? He lives on my street. You all probably thought he up and joined that weird cult, but that government agency took him and made him into—"

Jennings wants to put the gun down, but he's still fearful. "But—"

"Trust me, he's not evil like some of the others." I walk towards the still unconscious Astid. "She's not with them, either. Astid's on our side." I point to Cadence's lifeless body. "They turned Cadence into a black-eyed kid too."

Marcus looks absolutely like himself, except for his big black eyes. A million questions run through my mind about what will happen to him, but I'm still too fuzzy on everything myself to even begin to wonder.

"They strapped me down," Marcus says as he rubs his head. "I tried to get up. Then they injected me with some stuff to make me sleep. I remember one of those scientists saying something about me not having a normal, functioning brain to begin with."

I laugh at him. I just can't help myself.

"I'm glad you're finding this amusing." Detective Jennings puts his pistol away. "But we have a situation here that I'm not entirely sure how to handle." He looks at me with nervous eyes. "You and I both killed government agents. I'd say we're pretty screwed."

I crouch down next to Astid and pull the dart from her arm. She's still out cold. I'm about to ask Marcus to help me lift her up when Lisa's thoughts interrupt me.

I want to go home. I just want to go home, Lisa thinks to herself.

"Lisa?"

Lisa's eyes swing all around, and she's looking for Astid's brother.

"Don't worry about the other BEKs," I tell her. "They're not here. We're safe now."

I leave Astid and start to go to Lisa. She runs toward me and embraces me. Her tight hug feels good, and I nuzzle her hair resting on her shoulder. She releases me, and we all stare at one another— Marcus, Detective Jennings, Lisa, and me.

Now what do we do?

"Can I just go home now?" Lisa keeps her arms around me. "I just need to get out of here."

"Yeah, you can go home now," I say.

42

MAVERICK

ASTID'S STILL KNOCKED out and laying on Lisa's couch. She looks so peaceful, yet dirty from the mud she had fallen in. It still freaks me out not seeing any sign of her breathing.

"Are you sure she's not dead?" Lisa asks again.

"She's not dead," I reply.

Detective Jennings sits down in the recliner across from the sofa. He places both of his hands on the graying tight curls on his head, and his mind swirls with more questions.

Marcus stands next to the open doorway between the living room and the hallway. He's pacing, lost in his own thoughts. Lisa checks all of the windows and doors to be sure they are locked up tight. She already set her house's alarm system when we first arrived, and she looks like she's preparing for the zombie apocalypse.

Jennings takes a deep breath before saying, "Okay,

let me get this straight. A secret government sector of some sort created these things—the Black-Eyed Kids —that escaped. And now they're trying to get them back to this Level 6 place."

I nod. I don't know what else to add. "You got it."

"I'm not so sure I'm too terribly happy to know you aren't a complete psychopath. I think that would be easier to deal with," he says. "This town is already on red alert. They think the cult that passed through has something to do with Tarick and your mother's death and Cadence and Marcus' disappearance. On top of that, I'm pretty sure that secret government agency will order all of us dead."

"Man, what are we going to do now?" Marcus asks.

He blinks and the black eyes become shiny under the dull light in the house. Marcus still holds the gadget that put him on the ground. He turns it over in his hand. He had taken it straight from Wilson's pocket before we had left. He's definitely sharper than before.

"We have four dead bodies back at the barn, and one of them has my bullet lodged in her, so I'll have to report this, but I'm not quite sure what to say. What will the medical examiner say when they do an autopsy on Cadence?"

"Maybe this is the perfect way to expose them," I say. "Let the public know of their existence and the government cover up."

"Maybe, but that would mean exposing Marcus

and the other one as well." Detective Jennings points toward Astid's sleeping form. He craves a beer right now. "Is that what you really want?"

We both glance at Marcus who is still shaken up.

"I don't want to be involved," Lisa says, walking into the room. "I want this to be over and go on with our lives again."

"That may be easy for you, but I don't think I can go back home like this," Marcus points to his face. "I'm not sure what they did with me, or why I didn't turn out like Cadence, but I can't face my mom with my black eyes. I'll end up wanting to suck the life out of her."

Marcus bolts towards the kitchen just as he lets out a heavy sob. I've never seen the guy cry, ever. And it's unnerving to see. And it pushes Lisa over the edge too. She's about to lose it.

Jennings gives Lisa a reassuring look. "I think you're okay. But the rest of us aren't so lucky. I killed one of their agents, as did Maverick. Marcus is one of their lost guinea pigs. They want Astid, her brother, and another BEK. Out of all of us, Lisa, I'd say you've got the least to worry about."

Lisa's somewhat relieved, but she's worried about me and Marcus now.

"I haven't called any of this in yet, so I bought a little time." Jennings shakes his head. "I was so sure I'd have a pretty solid plan thought up by now."

I check on Astid again, but she's still unconscious.

There must have been some kind of heavy duty drug in that dart.

"Sorry, Detective," I say. "I know it's a pretty big mess we're in."

Jennings sighs again. "I was just going back to the barn to snoop around again, try to find more evidence of the rash of disappearances in town." He frowns in my direction. "I honestly thought you were part of that cult, Maverick. I thought you had something to do with your mother's death, and that you'd eventually lead me to the rest of them. Boy was I wrong."

I chuckle sarcastically. "Truth is stranger than fiction, right?"

"You said it." Detective Jennings gets to his feet. "I'm going to go back to the barn and check everything out. After that, who knows. We'll just have to face the music."

"What about us?" Lisa asks.

"Just sit tight. Keep the doors locked and don't step out of this house." Jennings moves towards the door and puts one of his business cards on a small table. "Call me if you need anything. Otherwise, I'll be back first thing tomorrow morning."

He opens the door, after Lisa punches in the alarm code, and gives us one last reassuring look before stepping out. Once the door shuts, Astid begins to stir. I reach towards her with my mind, but she's still out.

"I'm really worried about Marcus," I say while

locking the door. "I've never seen him like this. If I were him, I'd go totally crazy right now. They turned him into a freaking BEK, and now he can't ever go back home."

Lisa shakes her head, and it looks like she might cry again. "It's horrible. I feel so bad for him."

From the kitchen, Marcus' yells, "Hey guys, I'm starving!"

My heart drops into my belly, and Lisa actually gasps out loud.

Marcus pokes his head into the living room. "You have any of those pizza rolls in the freezer? Or maybe a Hot Pocket?"

43

ASTID

THE MORNING GLOW through the gap in the window's curtains wakes me, and my mind still feels like it's floating on a cloud. Maverick is sleeping in a chair, and Lisa's down the hall in her room. Marcus rests on the floor in a sleeping bag.

I focus on Marcus' dreaming mind. His brain functions much as my mother's did when she was alive. They tried to alter him at Level 6's laboratory, but the conversion must have gone awry somewhere. He is a hybrid, like my mother.

The rest of Marcus' life will be filled with trying to fight off the craving to feed.

I replay the events at the barn as best I can remember, and I'm relieved that we're all still alive. I know I must have missed a lot, but Kren and Garn are still out there. I must go find them. I'm about to rouse Maverick when a wave of emotion hits me.

Lisa's crying.

I move silently around the boys and head toward Lisa's room. Her thoughts become clearer the closer I get. She's worried about what will happen to her, but she's mostly concerned about her parents. She cares deeply for them, and she wonders if the government will come for them all. All of these strange events have robbed her of her normalcy. Perhaps forever.

"Lisa?" I ask her with my voice before I open the door. "Can I come in?"

"Y...y...yes." Her timid response echoes the fright that overtakes her. *Oh God! Oh God!*

I open the door slowly. "I won't hurt you, I promise."

My reassuring words have little effect on her. Her bed is rumpled, and she leans against a pile of soft pillows.

"I know," she says, and wipes her tears from her cheek.

Once she stares at me, the scene from the previous day replays in her mind in a flash. I see me laying on the ground and Cadence being stabbed by Marcus. Maverick's about to be shot, and that's when the detective shows up and kills the female agent.

No wonder Lisa's on edge. She was nearly killed, along with Maverick. I can't believe I missed all of that.

I sit next to her. "I'm sorry."

She nods. "Astid, what will you do now?"

Lisa remembers me taking Ronald's life and seeing the look of pure fury in my eyes after being forced to kill him. Lisa's still terrified of me yet feels sorry for me.

I need to find my brother and his followers and put a stop to them. After that, I'm not sure. One day, I would like to put an end to Level 6 and their ghastly experiments. I watch the sun shine into the room grow brighter each moment.

"Marcus is pretty messed up now, isn't he? There's no changing him back, is there?" she asks.

No, I don't think changing back is an option for him. Yes, his life will not be the same, I fear. He will suffer greatly, and, more than likely...well, let's not think about it. I rise and go to the door.

"Maverick isn't going to be able to stay here, is he?" Lisa says just as I'm ready to close her door.

Maverick is too stubborn for his own good.

I hope not, I lie.

Lies are funny things, they come so easily to those with strong emotions. Humans lie all the time, but it's not something that I've ever done before now. For once, I think I understand the reasoning behind it.

She turns over on her bed and faces the window away from me, but her thoughts are as clear as the blue sky on a cloudless day. *There's nothing I can say that will keep him here.*

44

MAVERICK

THE SOUND OF the house's alarm system blaring rouses me from sleep, and Lisa punches in the code to silence it.

I jump off the chair and rush to the open door. "What happened?"

Detective Jennings is standing there, covering his ears.

Marcus is still on the ground, sound asleep. Unbelievable.

"I forgot to deactivate the alarm system," Lisa says.

The eardrum-piercing alarm stops. That's when the phone rings, and she rushes past me to answer it and give the monitoring service a verbal okay along with a password.

She hangs up and goes back into the living room. Detective Jennings follows her in.

The couch is empty, the quilt laying on the floor.

I'm in a wild panic, and I'm about to run out the front door to look for Astid when she suddenly appears in the doorway to the kitchen. I thought for sure she had run away again.

Astid smiles. *It's good to see you.*

Lisa is full of a thousand emotions all at once, and it's draining to be able to sense all of them. I'm not sure this whole mind-reading thing is for me. I think I liked it better when I couldn't see what a woman was thinking. Her emotions are sure on overdrive and feel like they all take a ride on the same roller coaster.

She thinks me and Astid have something going on.

"They were all gone." Detective Jennings plops down onto the recliner he sat in yesterday. "It's like it never happened."

"Who?" Lisa asks.

I already know the answer.

"All the bodies were gone when I went back to the crime scene," Jennings says. "They were swept away, without one trace of anything ever happening there. I almost came over here again last night to tell you, but I needed some time to myself to figure things out."

Marcus sits up and looks at us in the living room. I still can't get over the change in his eyes.

"So, Level 6 sent in someone to cover it up," I say. "But, they didn't come here, so they must not know about Lisa. Or at least don't care."

Lisa is still full of fear and doubt.

"So much for exposing them, though," Jennings says. "I feel as if I've just entered an episode of the *Twilight Zone*. I couldn't sleep last night. I kept thinking they'd send some assassins to get me or something. But no. Nothing. These secret government people give me the creeps."

"Tell me about it," Marcus chimes in.

Detective Jennings stares at Astid, and worry seeps into his thoughts. He wants out of here, and fast.

"Well, I suppose we can try to go back to our normal everyday lives and hope not to get noticed." Jennings sits back in the recliner and looks up at the ceiling fan. "All the weird things in town are being blamed on the cult."

"I don't think it's that easy," I say. "I feel like…I don't know. I just feel like I can't let this go. Tarick, my mother, and Cadence are dead. And Marcus is some kind of weird BEK mutant." I glance over at my friend. "Sorry, man. No offense."

Marcus scrunches up his mouth and shakes his head.

Jennings blows out a long breath. "What do you have in mind?"

"I want to expose Level 6 to the world," I reply. "It's not right what they're doing, and people need to know. I first need to find out everything I can about them. Who knows what other messed up experiments they're doing."

"Maverick, they'll make you disappear if you even

try such a thing," Lisa protests. "Why can't we just go back to our normal lives and finish school?"

I turn toward Lisa. "There's no going back to normal here, but I understand you wanting to stay out of this entirely. You shouldn't have been dragged into all this anyway. But there's no going back for Marcus and me now. I want to know everything about Level 6 and bring them down." I turn toward Astid. "We are in this together."

"I was afraid you'd say that." Marcus crosses his arms. "I don't want to go back there."

"What can you tell us about where they took you?" Jennings asks Marcus.

Marcus closes his black eyes in thought. "They first took me and Cadence to some office building in town. They drugged us and strapped us down. After that, it gets really fuzzy. I do remember being wheeled into a plane. The engines kinda woke me up for a second, so wherever they took me was pretty far. I don't remember flying back, or much of anything after that until I saw you at the barn. That's when whatever the hell they did to me started to wear off."

"You know where Level 6 is?" Jennings asks Astid.

She shakes her head. *They moved their headquarters long ago. I have no idea where they relocated. They also have smaller, temporary outposts all over the country. All over the world.*

"So where do we start?" Marcus asks.

Astid continues with her mind. *When I traveled*

with Kren, we did have a place where we stayed. It is very far from here. We might find something there, but I doubt Kren and the others are still there.

We're all silent for a long time, trying to figure out our next move. Even Marcus is lost in thought.

I finally break the silence. "It's a starting point. Maybe we should go to the BEK hideout. It's a start, anyway. Before we leave, I want to go to Ronald's hotel room. Hopefully they didn't clear his stuff out."

Jennings shoots out of the recliner. "Who is Ronald in all this? I thought he was a family friend."

MAVERICK

W E LAY LOW for a few days, quarantined to Lisa's house. Jennings has been bringing the occasional fast food fix for us, which is a great treat compared to the cans of ravioli we've been surviving on. Astid eats up all the vegetables, and has learned that the cooked version is ten times better than the frozen stuff.

Marcus goes back and forth between depression and his normal, goofy self. At this point, I know he's hurting...and afraid. He's had a rough childhood, and even though he wasn't particularly close to his mother and brother, he longs to go to them. His joking is most definitely a way to cope with his tragedy. Marcus has had his entire life hijacked, but he's been handling it pretty good. Better than me if I were him, that's for sure.

After three days, Jennings has agreed to help us gather Ronald's things, if his stuff is still at his hotel room. Lisa decides to stay at her house. Things with her have been weird, but I decide to let her have all the space she wants.

At the hotel, all Jennings had to do was flash his badge and we got immediate access to Ronald's hotel room. Luckily, he had paid for his room by the week, and he had another couple days left. Marcus and Astid wait in the car.

As we're walking towards Ronald's room, I can't help but think of Lisa. She's been keeping her distance from all of us, actually, mostly staying in her room and blasting music in her ears to drown out her thoughts. But her emotions still ring loud and clear. She is scared and confused about everything. I don't blame her.

Earth to Maverick! Head in the game, Bruh. Head in the game! Marcus chimes into my head.

This mind reading thing is getting on my nerves.

Once we gain access to Ronald's room, Jennings sweeps through it and helps me gather all of his stuff, mainly consisting of one duffel bag and one computer case. At least the guy traveled light. We leave quickly because the clerk at the front was becoming a bit uneasy, wondering if he should call his supervisor.

We then stop near my house where I check out Ronald's black Lexus. Amazingly, he'd left the keys inside the ignition. I get inside and start it up. Poor Ronald. Without his sacrifice, we'd all be dead.

Astid and Marcus ride with me since they know

that Jennings still feels uneasy being in their presence alone.

Sitting behind the wheel of Ronald's car, images of his last moments hit me like a bolt of lightning. Watching his life drain before my eyes is something I will never forget.

We follow Jennings to the pharmacy. He signals for me to wait. It's yet another opportunity to sit quietly in Ronald's car and replay everything in my mind again. Marcus, incredibly, doesn't say a word, and Astid is only thinking about finding her brother.

After several minutes, Jennings leaves the pharmacy, and we drive over to Lisa's house again.

We pull up to Lisa's house and follow Jennings to the door. He rings the doorbell, and once again, I'm starting to freak out. I think just the idea of going up to a door is always going to trigger that fear in me for the rest of my life.

Lisa lets us in, and we go straight to the dining room and turn on Ronald's laptop. It's pretty clean, with several folders consisting of spreadsheets. Luckily, one spreadsheet is nothing but passwords for his accounts, including his email.

"Look at this." I point toward the spreadsheet that lists all of the supposed sightings of BEKs. "He kept information on BEK killings in cities all across the country."

"Ronald was a very detailed man," Jennings says.

I close the spreadsheet. "Ronald is part of a large organization, one with resources and more importantly, information. Maybe if I can connect with his people without scaring them off, they can help us."

I open his email and see several messages from one guy by the name of Beck. I open the most recent one.

Ronald,

No word from you in a while, need status update. High activity reported in the southern region. Send update soon. Will be in touch.

Beck

"It's a start," I say. "If we need to expose Level 6, we will need to know everything about them. Ronald's group seems to be the experts on BEKs, but I don't think they are aware of how deep the government's involved, or at least Ronald wasn't."

"So, you're planning to search for the other BEKs?" Jennings asks.

"I'm not going!" Lisa is standing in the doorway between the dining room and the kitchen. "I can't do it, Maverick. My parents will be home in a few days, and they need me."

I leave my chair and go over to her. I touch her cheek and look into her eyes. "I know. But I have to go."

"But why? Why can't you stay here with me?" Lisa fights back tears, and her surge of emotions takes my breath away.

I pause before telling her, "So much has happened, and I just can't pretend it all away. I mean, look at me. I can freaking read minds now. What is that all about? I have too many questions that need answers. And Level 6 has taken away a huge part of my life ,and I just can't let that go."

She breaks away from me and scurries back toward the kitchen so I won't see her crying.

Astid walks over to me and gives me a weak smile. *Lisa needs more time to heal. She will be fine.*

"I'll just have to make sure to call her as often as I can while I'm gone," I say.

"That reminds me," Jennings says to me. "Give me your cell phone, Maverick."

I give it to him, and he throws it on the ground and crushes it. The glass shatters.

Marcus drops to his knees, picking up the remnants of it, holding them up in the air. "NNNOOOO! Why? Why would you do this?"

We all stare at him, and I start to laugh. He knows how to ease the tension in the room like no one else I've ever met.

Jennings rolls his eyes and hands me a new phone with an envelope full of phone cards.

"This pay-as-you-go-phone is untraceable," he says. "It has my new number programed into it." He holds up an identical one. "Also untraceable. We still need to be careful when we communicate with each other with the government tracking or listening in on our calls."

Marcus snatches it out of my hand, caressing it as if it's a tiny little baby kitten, and then kisses it. "I will love it, and kiss it, and take care of it. Seriously, bro, this is awesome! We will be like super-secret spies or something." Then his smile fades, and his kidding around dissipates. "But if your plan involves us tracking down black-eyed kids and stuff, I'm not liking that idea."

"Well, that's why I have you, partner." I slap him on the shoulder. "You will be my bodyguard."

Marcus puffs his chest up. "I like it, but I want a black suit with a tie and everything, just like the Men in Black. Oh, and a new code name."

I'm relieved that Marcus has kept a good portion of his personality when he crossed over from human to monster. The guy is hurting big time, but he's still trying to put on a happy face. Poor guy.

"That's it! We can call it Operation Monster Mash!" Marcus raises both arms into the air. "Alright, amigo. I got your back."

Jennings keeps a straight face. "Is this guy for real?"

"Afraid so," I say.

"Oh, and here." Jennings hands me a wad of cash.

"Cops make some big-time bank!" I have no idea how much money I'm holding, but it looks like a lot. "I can't…"

Jennings lets out a sharp laugh. "Please! It's what was rolled up in one of Ronald's socks from the hotel room. You're going to need it." Jennings points a waving finger at me. "Just please don't spend it all in one place."

I glance toward the kitchen. "Keep an eye on Lisa for me, okay?"

"I will," Jennings says. "And I'll do what I can from my end. I don't think I'm ever going to stop looking over my shoulder from now on. I'm just going to assume Level 6 is spying on me all the time." He gives my hand a firm shake. "I'll watch over Lisa for you."

Just for kicks, I push my mind outwards. Maybe if government agents are watching us, I can sense them. I'm not sure if I'm capable of that kind of power, but I try anyway. I sense nothing, but that doesn't mean a thing.

"Thanks." I release Jennings' hand.

The detective is sincere, that much I do know. In fact, there's no way anyone will be able to lie to me again. I hope I get used to this telepathy thing.

"Tell me about it," Marcus says. *This trip is going to be one crazy ride.*

"We can head back to your house one last time," Jennings suggests. "You should pack your stuff, but you got to be quick." The detective pauses and drops his head. "And Maverick, your mother's funeral is this afternoon." He puts his hand on my shoulder. "What do you want to do?"

When Jennings told me about my Dad coming into town three days ago, and how he took charge of Mom's arrangements, I wanted to go to him right then, but I decided to stay away. Dad has to deal with her death and my disappearance. That can't be easy for him, but I can't get him involved. Being connected to me has proven to be dangerous.

I want to attend Mom's funeral, but Level 6 might be there, and things could get ugly. If they wanted to haul me in, they could pretty easily do it at any moment. For all they know, the BEKs did me in, just like all their other victims. If that's true, I can't take the chance that they learn that I'm actually alive.

"I want to go, but maybe not make an actual appearance," I say. "Does that make sense?"

Jennings nods. "We'll go but keep our distance."

We gather Ronald's things, and Lisa comes rushing out of the kitchen and crashes into me, holding me tightly before letting me go and running back down the hall to her room.

I hear her thoughts in my head. *Maverick, I love you. Come back to me.*

Astid must be reading my mind. She flashes me a quick look of understanding. She's been fairly quiet these last few days, but I do get fleeting images and thoughts from her. Her brain doesn't work the same way ours does. She sympathizes with our emotions and feels for us, but she's also able to block a lot. Just when I'm on the edge of breaking into her deep thoughts, an internal wall kicks me out.

You have to teach me how to do that, I mentally tell her.

She smiles and nods. *I know Lisa means a lot to you. I will do all in my power to make sure you return to her. That's my promise.*

Marcus, Astid, Jennings, and I walk out into the front yard, and I look back at the front window and see Lisa staring at me.

I love you too, Lisa. I've loved you since elementary school when I pushed you down on the playground. I'm so sorry it took this long to find you, only to lose you forever. Stay safe.

I wave to her, knowing I'm not able to send my thoughts to non-telepaths, and I feel like a coward for not actually telling her how I feel. It's one thing to hear her emotions so clearly, but Lisa can't hear my thoughts.

Marcus sniffles and pretends as if he's wiping a tear away. "I love you too, bro."

I give him a soft punch to his arm and look up at Lisa's window. She's still watching me, and she waves goodbye. This may very well be the last time I see her face.

"So much for senior year," I say half-jokingly.

Marcus is dead serious when he says, "So much for the rest of our lives."

MY HOUSE'S front door is unlocked, and the living room is a mess. The ripped furniture leans on its side, and paperwork scatters the floor. Level 6 has been in here for sure. I'm even more pissed off now. It's not enough they had to kill Mom, but they had to come back and ransack our house.

Astid remains inside our car, which idles in the driveway, but Marcus follows me into my house and lets out a heavy sigh.

"Bro, they totally went through your stuff."

I zip open my backpack and go to my room. My drawers are still pulled open and my clothes are now on my floor. Papers, books, pictures…everything has been dumped on my bed. I punch the wall before picking up some of my things and stuffing them into my bag.

I grab a bunch of socks and underwear, along with some shirts and another couple pairs of jeans. Before I leave, I take one final glance at my room and shut the door.

Marcus moves to the kitchen, and I can hear him opening the fridge. Can't blame him, actually. My stomach growls. Not sure if I'm hungry or if I'm just so upset about leaving everything behind.

Mom's bedroom door swings wide open and I step inside. Level 6 was in here, too. I step over her undergarments on the floor and go to the bed. Underneath a pile of papers, I find a picture of the three of us. I was probably six years old, and I laugh at how tiny I looked. I kinda looked like a Muppet. But Mom is so pretty, and her smiling is how I want to remember her. Dad's arm is draped around her, and they look genuinely happy. I wonder what happened to that love they once shared.

I pick up the picture, remove the photograph from the frame, and slide it into my backpack. I close my eyes and silently vow to make Level 6 pay for what they did to her. What they did to all of us.

Marcus greets me in the living room with a plastic bag full of food. He's munching on some chips and waiting for me by the front door. "Ready?"

I pull my backpack closer against my back. "Yeah. Let's go."

WE PARK JUST outside the cemetery. Jennings pulls up right behind us and remains inside his car.

"Just wait here for me," I say to the others before stepping out.

I walk through the open entrance while scanning my surroundings for any sign of Level 6 agents, but it looks clear. Astid had reached out with her mind and assured me that the government spooks weren't in the immediate area, but it never hurts to be careful. I walk past all the headstones and mentally prepare myself to see Mom's funeral.

After walking down a narrow sidewalk, I spot a gathering in the distance. I carefully make my way towards them, but I don't recognize any of the people at the funeral.

I make a left turn and walk up a steep hill. Towards the very rear of the cemetery is another group of mourners. They're pretty far away, so I decide to cut through the gravestones to reach a small cluster of trees near the funeral.

As soon as I'm about fifty yards away, I quickly recognize Dad. He's wearing a navy blue suit and sunglasses. Tarick's parents stand next to him. Then I spot Marcus' mom. Many of the people are Mom's coworkers. Mom's gray and silver casket hovers above the ground on some kind of metal platform. Her favorite flowers, lilies, sit on both sides of the casket, placed on stands.

After I wipe my wet face with my hands, I see Dad turn towards the sky. Looks like he's saying a prayer. I want to run to him, let him know I'm okay, and that I'm not part of some religious cult. But I can't do that. I can't have him end up like Mom.

My hand grips the tree trunk and tightens until I feel the rough bark pierce my skin. I almost reach out to Dad with my mind to read his thoughts, but I decide not to. What good would it do? I already know what's on his mind just by watching him.

Despite the divorce, he and Mom still got along okay. She had gone through a bout of depression when he remarried, but they never yelled or fought. Not in front of me anyway.

Maybe I should leave a note for him back at the house. But what if Level 6 goes back there again? Maybe the town thinking that I've been kidnapped or joined up with a cult is for the best. The truth is too dangerous. Who knows how far Level 6 will go to keep their secrets.

The minister continues speaking when I decide to give Mom's casket one final glance.

I love you, Mom.

I pull my t-shirt up to my face to wipe away my final tears. That's it. No more crying. Anger is my ally now. My fury is so fierce, that it's almost calming. I've already taken a life, which was declaring war on Level 6. I'm way past the point of no return.

I turn away from Mom's funeral, go back up the hill, and leave what's left of my family and my old life behind.

46

MAVERICK

"YOU OKAY?" JENNINGS asks me as I exit the cemetery.

I nod. "My dad's there."

Marcus and Astid get out of the Lexus and walk toward me. They're both uneasy, not sure of what to say.

"Your mom was there, too," I say to Marcus.

He takes a deep breath. "Wish I could say goodbye to her and my brother one last time." Marcus' black eyes threaten to water. "But there's no way. Not like this."

"I know." My lips tighten, trying to hold back any more tears from falling. "I wanted to go to my dad, but the more distance we put between us and them, the better. We can't drag them into all of this, too."

"I have at least fifty messages from your father," Jennings says to me. "It won't be fun having to give him the runaround, telling him that we are investigating the whole religious cult-thing, but you're right. It's for the best. While you're gone, I'll keep you updated with what's going on around here."

"You think we'll ever be able to come back home?" Marcus asks nobody in particular.

I know there's no way we're ever coming back. "Maybe," I whisper. "If things work out, maybe we'll be able to return."

Jennings flashes understanding in his dark eyes and reaches out to shake my hand. "Good luck. Just don't get yourselves killed, alright?"

I take his hand and give it a firm grip. "And you promised to watch over Lisa. Can you also keep an eye on Marcus' mom and my dad?"

"Sure," he replies. "If I don't get a call from you in three days, expect a call from me."

Jennings shoots us one final smile before getting in his car and driving away.

I get behind the wheel of Ronald's Lexus and start the engine. Astid gets in the backseat and Marcus rides shotgun. Despite my determination, there's still an ounce of hesitation in the thought of leaving home for good. I grip the steering wheel and I think of poor Ronald who probably spent countless hours in this very seat. I wonder what it felt like for him to leave home after his wife and son were killed.

I put the car in drive and hit the gas. No one says a word as I maneuver away from the cemetery, drive onto the main street, and head for the highway.

47

ASTID

THE MAP OF North Carolina spread across Marcus's lap looks positively medieval. I can't imagine how anyone can possibly navigate with ease using one of these things. I've never had to retrace my travels, as Kren always took us forward. He always led and I followed.

"Where did you say we needed to turn?" Maverick asks.

"Bro, we're lost," Marcus says. "This dirt road isn't even on the map."

It's a few more miles. I scoot closer in the middle of the backseat so I can see more clearly out the front window.

"We're going to run out of gas in the middle of nowhere and be eaten by wild, hungry bears. I just know it." Marcus crumples the map into a ball, and his lips squeeze tightly together. "Why didn't Ronald buy a navigation system? This is a Lexus for God's sake."

"We're not lost, idiot," I say with my mouth, and Maverick laughs.

Marcus lifts his black sunglasses and stares at me, his abyss of blackness seems lighter than mine. "You sound weird when you talk out loud."

"Man, we are wearing off on her. She called you an *idiot*." Maverick laughs once again. "Insults are so much better when they're spoken."

I smile. The long hours spent on the highway during the previous day has all loosened us up a little. With Kren, I was always on guard. Even when I trusted him most, I still did not truly trust him. However, I trust Maverick. Surprisingly, I even feel comfortable with Marcus.

Despite that, I still guard my mind. Being in close contact with others who are able to tap into my thoughts has caused an ache in my head since my energy has been used to block their efforts.

Marcus doesn't delve too deeply, but Maverick has tried a few times. He's more interested in my past than what I'm willing to share at this time. Some things are better left buried and forgotten rather than brought back to the surface.

I trust these two, more than I've ever trusted anyone in my life. But they have no idea what they're in for in the coming days. I feel guilty for not trying harder to talk Maverick out of doing this, but I find comfort that I'm not on this journey all alone.

Marcus slides his shades back over his eyes and crosses his arms. "Well, I may be the least likely to win at Jeopardy, but I'm not the one that got us lost."

"We have been on this dirt road for a very long time, Astid," Maverick says. "Are you sure this is the way?"

Yes. Our refuge is remote to prevent Level 6 or other humans from finding us. This was home for a long time.

I stare at the tall firs that line both sides of the road. Their colors have already begun to change, and that means the weather will be cooler soon. I close my eyes and extend my powers, searching for the others who might be nearby. I sense no one.

"Let's just say that there are a bunch of BEKs still here." Marcus looks at me. "They're not going to welcome us with open arms are they?"

I shake my head. *They will kill us. Which is why you won't be going with me when we get there.*

"That's comforting." Marcus leans back in his seat. "We barely escape one death and drive toward another. Bro, we'll be lucky to make it out of our teens at this rate."

"Won't they sense us when we get closer to them?" Maverick asks.

"There!" I point to an opening to the right. *Pull onto that road.* The short dirt path on the right widens enough for the car to maneuver into it, but Maverick cuts the engine off.

"You didn't answer my question," Maverick says.

I have been reaching out, trying to sense them. So far,

I've found nothing. I'll go through the woods for another mile toward the entrance of the cave, but first I need to travel north and check to see if any of their vehicles are still there. I think I can safely do that without being noticed.

"I'm not liking this plan," Maverick says with his hand still on the ignition key. "It seems to me that you are taking all the risk, and we did say we were in this together." Maverick turns his brown eyes on me. "We're supposed to just wait for you?"

We might be out of range for sensing the others, but they could also be putting up a mental wall. I believe that they have abandoned the shelter. I must first find out before we proceed.

"I'm liking Astid's plan just fine, thank you for asking," Marcus says with a grin. "I'm all for living another day."

Maverick starts the car and gets onto the dirt road. "Marcus, what happened to that manly confidence you had before we left. Bodyguard and everything?"

"I've been thinking and it dawned on me that this gig wasn't on my life plan," Marcus says.

"Your life plan?" Maverick asks.

Marcus says, "Yeah, the one we all had to do last year in that bogus AVID class, preparing us for our futures. You remember?"

Maverick chuckles. "If I recall, your life plan consisted of: One, marrying a rich chick. Two, marrying a rich chick. And three, marrying a rich chick's mother. You flunked your life plan assignment."

"The perfect life plan," Marcus says. "And nowhere on that plan was getting turned into a super freak and dying before I reach legal drinking age." Marcus suddenly becomes serious. "My life plan is pretty much down the toilet."

Their discussion about planning a life is juvenile, and I'm annoyed. *I'll be back in under an hour.* I shake my head and open the door.

"Wait!" Maverick steps out of the car and holds out his gun to me. "Remember, just like we practiced. You're faster than them. You can aim and shoot before they'll know what hit them."

When I take it, our fingers touch, and the jolt of energy flows through us. He waves his hand in the air to shake off the feeling.

Sorry, I tell him.

"Maybe you don't need a gun." He smiles. "Do you remember how to shoot it?" His eyes flicker toward the pistol in my hands.

We had just practiced yesterday. Since it was a better idea to stop for a few hours during the night so we could arrive here in daylight, Maverick had pulled into a secluded area off the highway. We all took turns practicing with the pistol.

Maverick unloaded it, but it did help to become accustomed to the weapon's weight while wielding it. But practicing with an empty gun and actually shooting it were two different things, Maverick had told us.

I nod and step out of the car with the gun in my hands. With one last look at Maverick over my shoulder, I start towards the tall mass of trees that cover the mountain.

Even though I had told Maverick that I needed to walk one mile to check for the vehicles, the hiding spot for the vans is about two miles away. I wanted to have as wide a range as possible in case Kren or anyone else is here, which I doubt.

After Kren and Garn had fled, they probably came back here to alert the others that it was no longer safe. To them I am compromised. A traitor to our species. Kren would portray me as a threat to everyone. He would only be partially right.

Kren is the one I need to kill.

What happens after that hasn't even played out in my mind. I cannot even begin to think what we should do after I take Kren's life force. Level 6 is still out there, hunting us and hurting innocents. No time to think about that now. I must focus.

My pace quickens, but my mind is on high alert. I stretch my limits and listen for any sign of anyone nearby. Nothing present but the animals that fear us, which scatter away as quickly as possible.

The landing comes into view, and just as I suspected...both vans are gone. The connecting kudzu vines that covered them under the tall trees swing openly in the air. Tire tracks lead down the path, so they must have left fairly recently. Kren and the others are maybe three days ahead of us.

I get back onto the beaten path, and the familiar site of the cave entrance comes into view. The boulder blocking the entrance would take several humans to move, but I push it to the side easily. My increased strength since taking Ronald's and Avion's energies will sustain me for several more days. Hopefully it's long enough to track Kren down.

Lacking life energy means certain death. I don't want to think about growing weak during my search for Kren, which means I will have to feed again. All those years and lives I took weigh on me, like that boulder smothering the earth. Avion deserved to die. Garn does, too.

Kren is the most deserving to meet his end.

The coolness within the mountain feels like home, but the silence becomes unbearable. My eyes adjust to the darkness, and then every visible crevice comes into focus. Everyone is gone. All of them. My brother took them all away, fearing for their safety. The few belongings that we had collected over the years are scattered about. They left in a hurry.

I step inside, and everything feels familiar yet alien to me. The part of the cave where I used to sleep is untouched, and I'm grateful they didn't ransack my things. I grab the only thing that means anything to me...Mother's red, dirty jacket. She wore it the day she was abducted and taken to Level 6.

Out of mercy, they let her keep it. Her jacket and

Kren…the only two links to Mother that I have left in the world. I put the jacket on and imagine Mother's arms around me. It fits me perfectly. I wallow in the temporary comfort before leaving the cave.

Marcus and Maverick come within the mental field I push out, and they're sitting silently in the car. Fear and worry emanates from them, and they hope that I return soon.

Maverick senses me first. I'm shocked. I'm two miles away, and he's able to weakly connect with my mind. His mental abilities grow stronger, and I feel his energy linger in my mind, pushing for information. Marcus might have been converted to be like me, but Maverick's abilities far exceed his.

This is something we had not discussed yet. Something must have happened when Kren had him in his grasp. How such power could have been awakened in Maverick is still a mystery to me.

Perhaps Maverick had potential to begin with.

Astid? Is everything okay? he asks with his mind.

Yes, I'm fine. They are gone, though. I'm fairly sure I didn't need to tell him that, as he was already connecting with my mind. I know he felt my thoughts when I became lost in my memories for a moment.

I turn back towards the empty cave. *There's nothing here that tells me where they have gone. I'm sorry.*

At least you have your mother's jacket now.

I pull her jacket tighter around my body. It is strange to share such intimate thoughts with another…especially a human. *Yes. That is my consolation. But now what do we do? I don't even know where to begin to search for Kren. There are many others scattered all over, but we had little to no contact with the other factions.*

Maverick's mind turns to Ronald's computer. *We still have our one lead. It will have to be good enough. You should make your way back to the car, and we'll talk about it.*

I take one final long, hard stare at what had been my home for five years. If I could destroy the cave, I would. There's too many dark memories here, and I'll be relieved to leave it all behind.

I return to the narrow path and make my way back to Maverick and Marcus. Despite knowing that the others are gone, I still continue to mentally scan my surroundings, just in case.

Once I make it back, Maverick has the computer on the hood of the car and shows me the screen.

RONALD,

Atlanta region a hotspot. Hurry to area, others will be sent as well. Red Top Mountain State Park – eyewitness sightings. Contact ASAP.

Beck

THIS IS where we are heading? I ask Maverick.

"Ronald found you, thanks to his network of

fellow investigators," Maverick replies. "And this is all we have to go on at the moment. I need to reply to this Beck guy so as to not make him suspicious, but I'm not sure if I should tell him I'm not Ronald or go on pretending to be him."

Marcus paces back and forth. "I know I'm the idiot of the bunch here, but seriously, I'm not sure about Ronald's club of geeks. We're already walking targets. I'm thinking that Level 6 has pretty close tabs on them, probably."

You are not an idiot. I apologize for calling you that earlier. I bow my head towards him. *And you have a very valid point.*

"My therapist was an agent," Maverick says. "She hypnotized me and probably pulled all kinds of information out of my head. Who knows how much Level 6 knows about everything, but I would put money on the fact that they know about Ronald and his organization."

Atlanta is our only lead. I glance back down at the email. *Maybe we can get some answers from this person named Beck.*

Maverick eyes me suspiciously for one fleeting second.

I lean towards him. *The next life I take will be Kren's, I assure you.*

"I think the closer we get to the BEKs, the closer we will get to Level 6," Maverick says. "I don't think we have much of a choice at this point."

Maverick's thoughts drift to the night that he

played video games with Tarick. Now he's thinking of his mother. He still cannot believe how much his life has changed in such a short amount of time. One minute he's a normal teenager looking forward to normal teenage problems, and a week later, his world is shattered by a simple knock on the door.

Marcus breaks the silence. "Well, one journey ends and another begins."

I turn to both of them, realizing that we have all been reading each other's thoughts. This will take some getting used to.

Atlanta? I ask them mentally.

"Yeah." Maverick points towards the car. "We need to get a GPS or something. Maps suck. We can't afford to be getting lost on our way to Atlanta."

Marcus gets into the passenger side and opens the wrinkled map. "I'm with you on that one. We need GPS and lunch."

A cool breeze sweeps through the valley, and a shiver runs through me. These boys have no idea what Level 6 is capable of. I do not appreciate their lackadaisical nonsense.

Maverick looks at me, having just glimpsed my thoughts. *We do it to cope. Especially Marcus.*

I get into the back seat and put up my mental shield. I want what Maverick wants—to destroy Level 6. Finding them will only bring us pain. Level 6, the origin of my life, was home to unspeakable evils.

And destroying it means going back.

MAVERICK

U SING THE NEW GPS we got at a Walmart just outside of Charlotte, I decide it's time to find a place with WI-FI and reply to Beck, saving what little connection we have left on the portable WI-FI device Ronald had. Beck's probably suspicious that Ronald hasn't replied to his email yet, which makes me think it's best to pretend to be Ronald when I email him back.

I exit the interstate, and after just two right turns, I pull into a restaurant parking lot. There's a sign in the window flaunting free WI-FI, so I kill the engine and grab the laptop.

"This looks promising," Marcus says with a yawn. "I'm thinking they have pancakes here."

The restaurant's logo includes a stack of pancakes, and my stomach rumbles. "I hope so."

Astid slides her sunglasses over her face and exits from the back seat. After stretching, she turns to me and her thoughts come to my mind. *So, will you answer Beck while posing as Ronald?*

"I think it's best to keep stringing this guy along. We still need to find out exactly where we're supposed to meet him." I reach back in the car and grab the charger. "We're a little more than three hours from Atlanta, so this is a good place to stop and wait for Beck's reply."

Marcus leads us into the restaurant, which looks more like a diner. It's mostly empty, since it's between lunch and dinner time. The hostess reluctantly takes us to a booth. She feels uneasy around our peculiar party, and after being seated, we all let out a deep exhale before I fire up the laptop.

After connecting to the diner's WI-FI, I go straight to the inbox. There's one unread email, and it's from Beck. I open it up and allow Marcus and Astid to read my thoughts as I read to myself.

DAMNIT RONALD, where are you? I left a hundred voice mails for you. I hope you're okay. Atlanta is crawling with spooks. I don't know what the deal is, but something big is happening here. Lots of government activity going on. Unmarked helicopters, agents walking around and asking questions.

Get your ass down here and give me a hand! I'm going to try your phone again.

.   .   .

I NOTICE that the email was sent just two hours ago.

"I'd better reply," I say out loud. "Otherwise, he'll know something's up."

Marcus tugs at his sunglasses. "What are you going to tell him?"

We need his location, Astid conveys to me.

My fingers touch the laptop's keyboard. "I'm going to put this Beck dude at ease. Help is on the way."

End of Book One.

To continue this series, check out Death Arrives!

ACKNOWLEDGMENTS

Death Knocks has been a book long in the making, consisting of countless hours of writing, research, and brainstorming, but wouldn't have arrived without the help from many wonderful people.

We'd like to first thank our families, who have been there for us, allowing us to spend our valuable time outside of our regular responsibilities in order to pursue our passions. We love you all very much.

We'd like to thank our editor, Todd Barselow, who helped us shape this exciting story, and is always a pleasure to work with.

A special thanks to Thebookbrander.com, who is the wonderful and amazing cover designer.

Thank you to Dominic Reyes for the outstanding job he did on the Death Knocks book trailer. Your talents are truly appreciated.

Our story has become stronger with the help of our gracious and fabulous beta readers and critique partners. Thank you to Ainsley Shay, Nanci Branson, Rebecca Puglisi, Kathleen Doyle, Lindsay Currie, Ruthann Frost, Sydney Aaliyah, Theresa Milstein, and Trisha Leaver. You all mean so much to us, and we couldn't have done this without every one of you.

Finally, we'd like to thank the readers who honor us by reading *Death Knocks*. Thank you! Thank you! Thank you!

ABOUT THE AUTHORS

Miranda Hardy writes literature to keep the voices in her head appeased. When she's not in her fantasy world, she's canoeing in alligator infested waters, or rescuing homeless animals. She goes to coffee shops to do most of her writing while drinking tea. Unable to reveal too much, she has the most boring super-power ever (hint: you have to be a close relative for it to work). She resides in south Florida with her two wonderful children, and too many animals to mention. Visit her at mirandahardy.com.

Jay Noel was born on an uncharted island some-where in the pacific and raised by elves and fairies. Okay, maybe not, but Jay was always known to be one for daydreaming. Jay was actually born in New York, but currently lives in St. Louis with his family. He had a pretty normal childhood, except for that one incident where he gave Jeff Glass a bloody nose and lip in the second grade. But the jerk deserved it! He also attended Southeast Missouri State University where he played NCAA Division I tennis and gradu-ated Magna Cum Laude. Jay has a degree in English and Education. Visit him at jaynoelbooks.com